FIGHTER'S FEVER

THE METALLIC SIEGE

RICARDO NAZAIRE

An entry for this book resides with the United States Library of Congress.

ISBN: 978-0-578-85233-1

Cover artwork and design by: D. Tsui, S. Mead, & M. Perez

Additional story artwork provided by: D. Tsui & E. Menzo

Additional editing: Team Nazaire, S. Wright & S. Zink, PhD.

Interior formatting: Mark Thomas / Coverness.com

TABLE OF CONTENTS

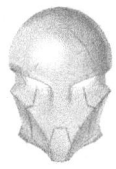

CHAPTER 1

"This is W-NJFM reporting live in Tortuga from outside of the Hasania Training Academy where a recent attack on the facility took place. Specific details on this attack have not been revealed, but given the number of instructors and trainees affiliated with the academy, it is safe to assume that there is a large number of casualties. Our thoughts and prayers are with the families at this time."

N ews outlets from across the region were spreading word of what took place on that fateful night. There was an immediate outpour of sympathy for those affected by the attack, as well as calls to hold those behind the chaos accountable for their heinous actions.

While the majority of those from the outside looking in thought that this terrorist attack was at the hands of rebels from the Tortuga, there were also those who insisted on digging deeper to reveal what they were really up against.

"What are you saying, Madam Chambers? Are you seriously suggesting that we don't do anything about this?" Beth objects. "How is that fair to us? Do you have any idea what kind of position this puts us in?"

"Beth, is that really the way to speak to Madam Chambers," Aya quietly warns. "Be mindful of your tone please."

"Who said this was a matter of what is fair? I understand how you must feel, but you need to understand that between the Agent Keyes incident and this recent attack on the Academy of all places, that this is bigger than all of us," Madam Chambers calmly explains.

"Having said that, I cannot in good conscience put you two in harm's way."

"With all due respect, what exactly do you have in mind for us?" a determined Beth asks.

"You are as insightful as always, Elizabeth," Madam Chambers thinks to herself. "These are, indeed, challenging times ahead of us," she says. "The last thing we can afford to do is lose our composure."

"The best course of action is to put aside all of our differences and reach out to one another as that is where our true strength lies." Madam Chambers takes a brief pause to collect her thoughts before continuing on.

"Then again, to accomplish that may be a little easier said than done. One can only hope for a miracle."

*

Meanwhile, in the quiet calm of the morning in the outskirts of the city, a young man tries to assess the recent turn of events.

"So, before I move forward, I just want a quick recap on a few things," an uncharacteristically doubtful Keenth asks Cory.

"Sure, I don't see a problem with that. Go right ahead, Keenth,"

Cory replies. "Whatever makes you feel comfortable, I suppose."

"Sure whatever," Keenth snaps as he paces back and forth. "So, you say that your name is Cory, correct?"

"That's right; it has been my name for as long as I could remember."

"And you, Cory, were sent by a sage named Haden?"

"I do recall sharing that with you, yes."

"And this all-knowing, all-powerful Sage, Haden, thought it would be in my best interest for him to send you my way?"

"I feel as though you are just rephrasing your questions at this point, but–"

"Withdrawn," Keenth says as he makes an abrupt stop. "That much I can take your word for, but there is something that I'm not so sure of, if I'm being honest here."

"And what would that be?" Cory replies, showing concern.

"Excuse me if I'm stepping out of line here, but are you sure you are a girl? I mean with a name like Cory Daken? Saying it out loud, it could leave a guy a bit confused. Oh, and while we're leaving it all out there on the table, that short brown hair cut doesn't help the situation much either because—"

"You do understand that I literally saved your life and, at the rate this is going, keeping you out of harm's way is looking like the biggest mistake I've ever made," Cory responds in an apathetic tone.

"You don't really mean that," Keenth replies. "The fact that your Sage sent you out to get me means—"

"People make mistakes all the time and Lord Haden would understand. I mean, you falling off of a cliff would be a pretty understandable accident. No one would ever have to know. No one would hear you scream. If that's the path you want to take, then just give me the word and I will be happy to oblige."

"Not to cut you off or anything, but that blue robe is a really, and I mean really good look on you. A bit retro for my taste, but it really brings out your eyes. Speaking of eyes, I've heard that they are a window to one's soul. Pretty interesting, right? W-wait, why are you walking away?"

"Because we've wasted enough time," Cory replies with her back facing Keenth. "Look, you don't seem like a bad person and all, but you really need to understand the gravity of the situation. The fact that a Sage is reaching out to you speaks volumes. Lives were already lost and I feel that if we don't take action, then…"

Cory pauses. Without realizing, she did not take into consideration how Keenth was personally affected by the attacks. Keenth Hedstrom is a seventeen-year-old who has spent the last several months attending the Hasania Training Academy.

Behind his dark blonde hair and soft, yet stern, brown eyes lay a young man torn. Anyone else in that situation would be going through a whirlwind of emotions. How Keenth would honestly express himself is beyond Cory or anyone else's guess.

"You know what? Never mind, let's just move forward," Cory suggests. "I can't promise that all of your questions will be answered, but I can definitely get us going in the right direction. All I ask is that you trust me on this. Please."

Without directly facing Cory, Keenth silently thinks to himself. It seems as though the realization of what happened had finally set in. He made his way towards her with an expression that was without fear or worry.

Keenth places his hand on Cory's shoulder, assuring her that he was ready and that was all they needed to press on. It seems as though for these two what is understood doesn't need to be explained.

*

Later that same morning, the focus turns to the remains of the Training Academy. At this point, the press and those without a need to know are removed from the surrounding area so that the investigations can be conducted without interference.

Even though Agent Jennifer Connors has no trouble as the Senior Intel Specialist of the LanTech Empire with the tasks at hand, it would seem that dealing with a certain someone would be one of her biggest hurdles for the time being.

"Our briefing ended over twenty minutes ago and you were nowhere to be found," Agent Connors calls out to the individual trying to sneak away from the area. "What do you have to say for yourself, Agent Fallon?"

"Oh, didn't see you there! Real quick, when you say Fallon, are you talking about me or my brother, David?" Agent Fallon playfully replies.

After all, people confuse the two of us more often than you think," Agent Fallon continues. "If it means anything, you guys could call me James if it makes it easier for everyone—"

"Excuse me, everyone. If the rest of you would excuse the two of us for a few minutes, Agent Fallon and I are going to have a little chat," Agent Connors responds, while motioning for him to follow her.

"So, it's safe to assume when you say chat, y-you mean the one way kind, right?"

"It seems to be the only kind you know, Agent Fallon."

After walking a considerable distance, Agent Connors *expresses* her thoughts to her subordinate until it seems as though the message is falling on deaf ears. Knowing that there were more important matters at hand, she promptly dismisses him, but not before he shares a few words of his own.

"Aren't you going to let me answer your question, Agent Connors?"

"Question? I told you a lot of things, most of which I can't repeat near children or the elderly, but I don't recall opening the floor for questions," Agent Connors hastily responds.

"Right, right. I could have sworn you asked me what I had to say for myself and I have one word for you: trainees."

"What are you getting at, Agent Fallon?"

"That's right, the trainees. Think about it: there was an attack on this Academy, but the building itself is still mostly intact. If the goal was to destroy the building, they had the time and means to do so to really get their point across."

"But where do the trainees even come in? We held a memorial ceremony for Agent Keyes hours before the attack took place. Between the security measures that we took prior to our arrival and when the attack took place, it would just make more sense to attack while we were there."

"Well, that is based on the notion that the taking the lives of LanTech Agents would have more of an impact. With all due respect, we should really get off of our high horse when it comes to—"

"It would be wise to watch your tone," Agent Connors replies. "This comes off as nothing more than a personal interpretation about what could have happened. What else do you have to go on?"

"The personnel database for the Academy. Between everyone there, the trainees are the biggest variable. Most of the guests departed before the attack took place and we can easily scope out the staff by their identification passes."

"But it doesn't stop there," Agent Fallon continues. "Each and every staff member has been accounted for. Though I wish I could say the same for the trainees," Agent Fallon says as he slowly looks down.

"Go on."

"I'm sure that this was covered during the briefings, but most of the deceased have the same cause of death which is smoke inhalation. The majority of them died in their sleep, almost as if there was an external factor involved."

"As far as the ones that were awake, it seems as though their defensive wounds suggest that they put up a struggle before being incapacitated."

"This goes beyond any rebel attack that we have ever encountered," a disturbed Agent Connors replies. The fact that this information was enough for her to lose her bearing said a lot about the complexity of the situation.

"But there's hope. From what we can tell, there are a handful of trainees that are still unaccounted for. My theory is that this is more than likely some sort of hostage situation with the attack being used as a distraction."

"Okay. I want you to come with me so we can move forward with this information. All of it," Agent Connors says as she heads back to inform the others. Before moving forward, she had to feel there was more to what Agent Fallon was letting on though.

"While I appreciate you decided to come forward with this, I can't help but wonder why you were so involved with these matters without sending things up the proper channels?"

"Ah, well you see, I had this theory and thought that I should just run with it."

"Well, what you need to understand is that everything falls on me when it comes to this investigation. Your tasks come directly from myself unless otherwise stated. Am I clear?"

"Crystal," Agent Fallon responds. "With my brother being a fellow Agent and all, it looks like I forgot where to check in. It's pretty funny if you think about it. Like I said, people confuse the two of us—"

"More often than you think," Agent Connors said, finishing his sentence. "I know Agent Fallon, I know…"

"E-Excuse me, Ma'am, but we have just received this message addressed to you," a LanTech patrolman frantically states as he approaches Agent Connors.

"Thank you," Agent Connors says as she activates the message in the form of a holographic memorandum.

"Patrolmen deliver messages to Agents all the time. Why is he so shaken up?" Agent Fallon asks.

"It wasn't the message that concerned him," Agent Connors slowly replies. "It was the sender. If I'm being honest, I can't say I blame him."

*

Much later that day, Keenth and Cory continue on their journey. It didn't take long for both of them to realize that they could truly trust one another.

Still, it wouldn't be much of a journey without its fair share of mishaps and shenanigans; a lesson that this pair would be learning sooner than they would expect.

"Keenth, it's dark, and we still don't have a plan when it comes to resting up. Do you think we should think of something before it gets too late?" an exhausted Cory asks Keenth as they continue down a forest trail.

"Nonsense! We're warriors! What is life without a little adventure," Keenth boldly exclaims, trying to boost their morale.

"Keenth, for the last time, I'm fourteen years old. Four-teen.

I understand that moving forward is important, but I also have a bedtime."

"Okay, you're right. Sorry about that. Hey, I know! You should try some of these grains that I picked up along the way. They don't taste too great, but they're better than nothing."

"Now that you mention it, I must've lost the rations that I brought with me during all of the chaos at the Training Academy. I'll take some, if you don't mind."

"I've got plenty, so take as much as you need!"

As they press on, the two begin to notice that their surroundings were a bit too familiar. Cory, naturally being an outdoors type of person, is surprised at the oversight that was made on their behalf.

"S-say K-Keenth. Is it just me or is it getting k-kinda warm all of a sudden," a flustered Cory asks. "And don't say it's because of my robe because you are sweating up a storm over there too."

"N-now that you mention it...I'm not feeling too hot either. I mean I'm feeling hot, j-just not that...S-screw it," Keenth says as he collapses on the ground.

Cory tries her hardest to rush to Keenth's aid, but her own movements are sluggish. Before she knows it, she begins to collapse as well. Fortunately, she was able stop herself by putting one knee to the ground.

"K-Keenth, w-where did you say you got these grains again? I d-didn't feel like t-this until...u-until...ah, s-screw it," Cory says to herself before losing consciousness.

A few hours later, the two are in the middle of the forest near a campfire adorned with flickering flames freely dancing under the moonlight.

Upon first glance, Keenth is under the impression that they are being graced by the presence of a good Samaritan. That, however, changes all too quickly when he realizes that they are both bound to a large tree.

"Cory! Cory, wake up," Keenth shouts, trying to get her attention.

"It looks like she'll be out for a while. That works out just perfectly because the two of us have some catching up to do," a mysterious woman says from beyond the woods.

"Who's there? Show yourself," Keenth defiantly shouts. "Let us go right now!"

"You are in no position to make any demands, my little Francis," the voice responds. "Not after what you've done to me. How you've betrayed—"

"W-wait, who the hell are you? I don't even know you—"

"Hush your little mouth," she replies as she places one of her fingers over Keenth's lips. "I know you've gone through so much, but your Vera is going to take very good care of you, my dear Francis."

"Francis? Have you hit your head or something? What do you want from me?"

"To be reunited with you! You were so distracted, playing around in your little Academy back there. But now that you are here alone with me, I will make sure we are never separated again!"

"You are a special kind of crazy lady! Let me and my friend go right now!"

"Crazy…Tell me, Francis," Vera says, while reaching for a small dagger from her tattered brown sash.

"Is it crazy to silently trail you from the Academy? Is it crazy to leave grains along your path that would cause you to lose consciousness? Is it crazy to have you both in an area where, if faced with this scenario, no one would be able to help you?"

"Yes. Yes, it is to all of the above. Absolutely crazy," Keenth replies, while trying to free himself from his binds. Realizing that was no use, he begins pleading with his captor.

"Listen, it looks like it's me that you want. So, please, just let her go. She has nothing to do with this."

"No, no, no! I won't have that," Vera shouts in Keenth's face. "She has everything to do with this! How do you think I felt watching this little vermin alongside you? Saving you, caring for you. That should have been me, Francis! That should have been me!"

Keenth realizes that Cory is still unconscious. After noticing that his sword and Cory's staff were beyond reach, he thinks to himself how he's completely out of options and truly at Vera's mercy.

"Vera, right? Look, I'm sorry. I'm sorry for everything that I must have put you though, I truly am. I know I don't deserve your mercy, but I truly, truly hope that you can find it in yourself to forgive me."

Vera thought to herself for a few moments which to Keenth felt like an eternity. From there, she walked towards the campfire and took a knee while responding to Keenth's apology.

"Francis...My dear Francis, I just want to say that I accept your apology, I really do. At the same time, I know that words can only mean so much," she says as she rises to her feet.

"What are you getting at?" an uneasy Keenth asks Vera as she slowly begins to approach him.

"Words don't hold much value these days. They can be taken back, misused, or misread without rhyme or reason. From that I came to understand that while words can leave you disappointed, actions are the only things you can hold true in this world."

Vera reveals that her dagger was used alongside the campfire with the purpose of branding an unsuspecting Keenth. To Keenth's shock,

Vera slowly reveals a carved letter V on her left forearm.

"I figured that since I have this on my arm, then it would only be right for this to be on one of yours too. Now tell me, is that crazy enough for you, my little Francis?" Vera asks as she makes her way back towards Keenth.

"No! Please just leave us alone," Keenth pleads to Vera's unforgiving ears as she raises her weapon. "You don't have to do this!"

"Again, going on and on with the words. It's time to give you a lesson worth remembering. One that will be carved into your skin for the rest of your—"

Before she could finish, a massive fiery explosion from the campfire shakes the surrounding area. Many of the trees are set ablaze.

"Francis! What have you done?"

"Ah, you're right! Of course! The guy tied up this whole time was clearly behind this, you genius!"

Before they could continue to bicker, a mysterious figure approaches through the flames unharmed. Puzzled by such an abnormal presence, Vera completely loses her composure.

"D-Demon! He's a demon!"

"Demon? Sorry lady, but you're dealing with the devil himself."

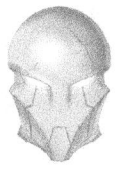

CHAPTER 2

J ust when it looked like Keenth's confrontation with Vera was reaching its boiling point, a mysterious young man enters the fray. But the answer to whether he is a friend or foe remains to be seen.

Brushing off his initial shock, Keenth focuses his sights on the warrior among the flames. From what he could tell, the young man was around Keenth's age, but his appearance and demeanor were worlds apart, with the young man adorned in a dark blue battle garb that was draped underneath a flowing, gray cloak.

His dark hair, while long and unruly, seemed to flicker synonymously with the wild flames that surrounded the area. Through his strong brown eyes, Vera knew that she was facing an individual with unwavering conviction.

"Does this devil have a name?" Vera asks, after seemingly regaining her composure.

"I usually don't share that kind of information so easily," the young man replies. "But maybe if you have what it takes to earn my respect—"

"His name is...Benjamin...Benjamin Palorro," Cory weakly states from a distance.

"Because earning my respect is something that...Could you not interrupt?" Benjamin angrily exclaims at the young apprentice. "Who the hell are you to reveal my name? Where's your sense of intrigue? Where's your taste for dramatic flair? Where—"

"Um, sorry, but where is your opponent?" Keenth asks out loud, causing Benjamin to fall into silence.

"Your arrogance will prove to be your downfall," Vera's voice echoes through the forest as she remains hidden from her opponents' sights. "At first, you appeared to be an impressive foe, but I will make short work of you so that Francis and I can finish our conversation!"

Before Benjamin can react and Keenth might object, a massive tree is hurtled towards them. Keenth and Cory, who were still firmly bound, were defenseless to the attack, but Benjamin stood fearlessly before the impending danger.

At what seemed to be the last possible moment, he swiftly raises his right arm before him causing a wave of violent, red flames to incinerate the projectile. Some of the flaming debris made its way to the ropes that were restraining Keenth.

As soon as he sees this opportunity, he uses all of his might to tear away his bonds.

After making a dash for his sword, Keenth realizes that Cory's staff is missing. He remembers that he's left a barely conscious Cory vulnerable.

"Could this night get any worse?" Keenth thinks to himself. That is, however, until he witnesses Vera dashing towards Benjamin, while hurtling sharpened branches.

"Let's see, let's see...Blue mage chick? Check. Flame wielding devil man? Got it. Nature loving sociopath? Why not? At this point, I should be okay with whatever life throws at me—"

Before Keenth could finish gathering his thoughts, he narrowly dodges one of Vera's branches heading towards him. Whether it was by instinct, luck, or a combination of both, this catches Benjamin's attention.

"That's the spirit, guy! Keep pressing on," Benjamin shouts a surprising act of encouragement.

As Keenth begins to pull himself back into reality, he notices that one of the enemy's branches is just mere inches away from his face. The reason why he isn't critically wounded is because Benjamin had appeared before him in a blink of an eye.

"What the hell are you standing around for?" Benjamin scolds Keenth as his tight grip turns a branch into ash. The thought of Benjamin moving in front of him before he could even react leaves Keenth in a state of awe.

"This is hardly the time for you to lose focus! You should be better than this!"

The two fighters found suddenly themselves immobilized by the ground below them. It appeared as though the earth beneath them was infused with Vera's energy.

"I apologize for using such primitive tactics," Vera says as she approaches them. "I just needed an opportunity for me to really take this seriously. I thought it would only be fitting to do things this way," she continues, while focusing on Keenth.

"Why is that? What are you getting at this time?" Keenth scolds as he struggles to free himself. "More importantly, how in the world did I manage to get trapped by you again? I can't help, but feel I have nothing but bad luck here."

"Hush! You're the reason why I went out and learned these abilities in the first place, Francis! It's pretty poetic if you really think about it," Vera replies as she summons two sharpened branches, wielding one with each arm.

"Now the question is who to start with first?"

Before Vera can continue, her branches combust, scorching her in the process. With both her ego and arms damaged, she quickly turns over to see the source of her anguish: Benjamin's arm pointed in her direction.

"How long has it been since I made my name here in Tortuga? Honestly, I can't care to remember. Either way, for years I've faced every challenge thrown my way dead in the eye," Benjamin continues.

"Most bouts ended in my favor and others not so much. It was through these seemingly endless battles that I pushed myself to be my absolute best."

Keenth listens as the surrounding flames began to roar. His initial view of Benjamin being an enigmatic warrior of sorts slowly, but surely, was blurred until he wasn't sure whether he was ally and foe.

Whether he knew it or not, there was now a hint of unease in Keenth's view of the young man.

"Be it as it may, I saw you from a distance, stalking the outskirts of the region like a vulture looking to reign down on its prey," Benjamin continues, as Vera remains speechless.

"The thought of you being able to best a Sage Apprentice and this guy over here got me pretty excited. But once I saw you firsthand, I had one thought and one thought only," Benjamin says as he looks down at his hands.

"A-and what was that?" Vera responds with fear. "What did you realize?"

"How wrong I was," Benjamin says as he clenches his fists causing a massive outburst of flames to eradicate the ground binding him.

"There is one thing that I can't stand and that is a challenge that isn't worth my time," Benjamin says as he concentrates the flames on his right fist.

Vera used what was left of her energy to desperately raise her arms to manipulate a wave of terrain toward her opponent. Benjamin rendered the dirt as harmless as dust in the wind.

Vera frantically attempts to retreat, but Benjamin appears before her. Keenth, who is now at a considerable distance from the two, rushes in their direction, while Benjamin begins to prepare the final blow.

"Be gone," Benjamin says as he begins to bring his fist down.

Keenth tries his best to mediate the situation, but it was far beyond words at that point. A wide-eyed Vera is in shock at the thought of her life facing such an abrupt end.

Suddenly, a massive quake causes Benjamin to be forcibly raised in the air. Once the dust clears, he realizes that the landscape has greatly changed and that he was standing on a stone plateau.

Surprised that Vera still had abilities to her disposal, the real shock comes when it is revealed that Cory is standing before their opponent.

"You're in my way, Apprentice. You have ten seconds to explain yourself right now," Benjamin angrily tells Cory.

"This battle is over, Benjamin. Your name is Vera, right? Leave this area and never show your face again," Cory states, while continuing to lock eyes with Benjamin. "There is no longer a threat here."

"That's not your call," Benjamin replies as he makes his way down to them. "You must have hit your head along the way because I could have sworn that I was the one who saved the two of you from her."

"You did and you have our thanks. But this is not the same Vera that you saved us from," Cory states as she continues towards them.

"I admire your optimism, but that kind of mindset just leaves an opportunity for a former foe to strike you down in the future. This does not seem very well thought out if you ask me," Benjamin replies, while inspecting one of the charred branches from the battlefield.

"Your goal is to become a more powerful warrior, isn't it? Then this is all the more reason for you to let this go. Slaughtering someone clearly incapable of being a challenge would be shameful. What's the point of being respected when taking the lives of those beneath you would be associated with your legacy as well?"

Benjamin carefully thought about her words as Vera slowly rose to her feet thanks to Cory's assistance. There was one more point that needed to be made before he decided how to proceed and Cory knew exactly what to say to erase any remaining doubt or hesitation.

"Rest assured that if she makes the decision to take advantage of this by attacking the helpless in the future, then I am willing to take full responsibility. I will personally act without any hesitation," Cory replies while patting a shaken Vera on the back.

Benjamin moves towards Vera and steps right in front of her so he could read her intentions. After a few moments but that felt like a lifetime, Benjamin tells Vera to flee and get counseling.

"To think that I was talked out of making an example of my opponent," Benjamin mutters to himself. "That Sage of yours must really be something. Your name is Cory, right? Go ahead and get comfortable because you and I are going to have a little chat."

"Hey, I'm still here guys," Keenth states, trying to re-establish himself.

*

With the full moon shining brightly, Beth Masterson stares at the high-end hotels of Tortuga through her window. She has always seen herself as a night owl of sorts, especially considering that she finds herself gathering her focus while the world around her rests. This night, however, it proves to be especially difficult to do so.

"Sorry to call you up this late, but I really wanted us to be able to speak freely about this," Beth asks as she motions for Aya to join her on the rooftop balcony.

"Not a problem. So, what did you want to talk about," Aya replies as she tries to keep her yawns at bay. "If you don't mind me telling me, is there any reason why you didn't bring this up earlier?"

"Well, you see…And don't get upset, but this is something that I discussed with Madam Chambers. We decided that the best plan moving forward is for you to return to headquarters as soon as possible."

"What? You're kidding me, aren't you? Don't you think I should have a say in this?" Aya immediately objects. "Besides even bringing seniority into it, you know that I'm just as much a part of this team as you are."

"I understand your frustration and no one is trying to take away what you mean to us. But we have to face the facts: these are very dangerous times and we won't risk allowing Madam Chambers to remain unprotected."

"But why me? We have plenty of capable members and I want the opportunity to make a difference out here. What good am I if I step out of the fight when we could use all the help we can get? I just don't understand."

"Don't underestimate your role here, Aya. We all have a part to play in this. You may not see it now, but hopefully you will come to understand this as well."

"Roles? It really is hard to connect with someone who is keeping me in the shadows. Being tossed to the wayside is one thing, but you won't even tell me where I stand in this"

"You're right, Aya. You are absolutely right. I will be staying behind. Between the Keyes Investigation and the attack on the Academy, we need some sort of presence in the area," Beth replied, but Aya looked less than convinced.

"Madam Chambers is going to provide me with some additional support so that all of our hard work does not go to waste," Beth replies, hoping to reassure Aya.

"Why is additional support needed? Shouldn't you be enough cover?"

"I shouldn't be sticking around this place for too much longer. Don't take this as me withholding information from you, but I think that call was made by someone way above our paygrade, my friend."

"I see, I see...Well, I appreciate you taking the time to tell me face-to-face. Having this head's up gives me some time to enjoy the region a bit more before I get my affairs in order," Aya says as she begins to make her way back inside.

"Oh, about that...You are kinda sorta slated to leave tomorrow."

"Well, if you put it like that...Damn it all. Can you just let me be great for once?" Aya sighs in defeat.

"Yeah, sorry about that. Try to get some rest. You have a long day ahead of you," Beth says with an apologetic smile.

*

Hours pass and as the sky awakens and Keenth and the others discuss recent events.

"I see, so that's how it is," Benjamin says to himself once Cory gets him up to speed. "Well, if it means anything to you, I think it would best if I moved alongside you two for now."

"Do you really think you can hang?" Keenth confidently chimes in. "After all, Cory and I go way back. That and three's a bit of a crowd, you know?"

"You do realize we just met yesterday?" Cory responds. "That and I think Benjamin is being respectful in trying to say that—"

"You're pathetic, Keenth. Terribly pathetic. I have every right to bring you back to what's left of that Academy because clearly you don't know the first thing about being in a battle," Benjamin states.

"If I could go just five minutes without someone trampling on my soul, that would be great," Keenth thinks to himself as before he attempts to remove the focus off him. "Right, whatever. So, what's the lay of the land, Benjamin?"

"Ah, right. I know these parts like the back of my hand. This is not really my style, but the best thing to do is hit you with a quick rundown before we go on. Keenth, take notes because I'm not repeating myself!"

"How did—," Keenth responds as he begins to stand up. "You know what? I'm just going to find a pen and paper…I am just too damn old to be talked to like this," Keenth mumbles to himself as he sits back down.

"Good. Anyway, let's talk about where we are. Hasania: The Land of the East. Our continent's symbol is the shield which represents honor," Benjamin explains. "There's way too much to cover as far as its history, so I'm going to focus on where we are and where we need to be."

"We are currently in Tortuga, a mountainous region in the northeast side of Hasania. Tortuga is known for its combination of both a rural and urban atmosphere and for having quite a few warrior hideouts."

While Keenth vigorously takes notes, Cory focuses on Benjamin's words because she is not all too familiar with this region either.

"For years, many warriors have been causing conflicts throughout the regions of Hasania with Tortuga being no exception. The respective regions have their own ways of handling warriors, but with Hasania being ruled by the LanTech Empire...they insist on providing their own means of handling situations."

"I remember one of my instructors teaching us about that," Keenth notes. "He said part of the reason that the LanTech Empire helped establish the Training Academy in the first place was a sign of good faith."

"Is that so? Sorry to break it to you but the majority of us out here feel otherwise," Benjamin responds.

"I can tell you firsthand that LanTech's true actions have caused tensions to increase at an alarming rate. These warriors, who they deem as rebels, have resisted LanTech and its methods for years, but it was only a matter of time before we got to where we are now."

"What does that mean for us?" Cory asks. "What do we do from here?"

"Well. I suppose those are questions more suitable for that sage of yours," Benjamin replies as he stares off into the trail ahead. "Truth be told, I didn't foresee something as chaotic as that attack on the Academy. But if there is one thing that I know, a storm is coming."

*

Later that same morning, a small silver air car stops at a quiet town outside of the Tortugan Capital City. Agent Connors steps out and begins to make her way, noticing the mixed reaction of the townsfolk on seeing a LanTech Agent in person.

"Black overcoats tend to draw attention around here. Perhaps you should have gone the casual route today." A woman quietly chuckles.

"My apologies, Madam Chambers," Agent Connors responds. "I made my way as soon as I received your message."

"No worries, dear. This should not take too much of your time."

"Right, of course. Speaking of which, and with all due respect of course, is there any particular reason why you wanted to speak to me? Given your status, I would think it would make more sense for you to have a meeting with the upper elites, like Agent Masterson or Van."

"Normally. I would agree with you, but I feel as though this is one of those exceptions where we keep certain politics out of the mix," Madam Chambers replies as she motions for them to sit on a bench overlooking the water.

"You probably could not tell just by looking at me, but I used to be young too. Well, many moons ago, admittedly. There was a time when I was young, ambitious, and looking to make a genuine difference for the people here and the rest of the world."

"Agent Keyes used to tell us stories about how you were such a thorn on his side way back when," Agent Connors quietly muses. "He said that even though he was a high ranking LanTech Agent, you never thought twice about speaking your mind."

"You're damn right I didn't! Even as the High Council of Tortuga, it felt like you Black Coats and I got along like oil and water for years. But through it all, I think we all had the same goal of keeping this region safe in mind, even if we did go about things differently."

"Madam Chambers, again with all due respect, treaties and peace talks can only go so far when it comes to dealing with these rebels. When it comes right down to it-"

"They only understand actions," Madam Chambers interjects. "You are more like Agent Keyes than you realize, Ms. Connors. The fact of the matter is, what we are looking at something bigger than warriors acting as they do. I know it and I believe you do as well."

"I don't understand what you are trying to get at, Ma'am…"

"What I am saying is that something is on the horizon. Unlike events of the past, this is not something we can just turn a blind eye to. I think maybe–"

"Maybe this is a conversation that should be discussed with the upper echelon and not out here between the leader of the Tortugan region and myself," Agent Connors replies.

"I arrived due to the urgency of the message, but I think that was poor judgment on my part. So, if you don't mind–"

"Actually, I very much do mind, young lady. Don't you find it just a little strange that your people have you, a mid-level Agent, leading the investigation on the attack of the major training academy in Hasania? An attack that is most possibly connected to the loss of a veteran Agent?"

Now I might sound like I'm just a rusty old relic, but if there is anything that I've learned throughout the years is that where there's smoke, there is fire," Madam Chambers continues. "It might be hard to realize, but the fact of the matter is–"

"Is what, Ma'am? What were you going to say?"

"Actually, I forgot what I was getting at. Maybe there is truth to me being an old relic after all. But look, the point is that we all need to be in this together if we want to stand a chance at what's ahead."

"Sorry, Ma'am, but you're wrong. Not a chance at what's ahead; it's already here."

"What are you trying to say, Agent Connors?"

"I probably sound like a broken record with this, but Agent Keyes always used to tell us that certain events may seem out of the blue at first, but they usually happen in patterns. So, if we really believe there is a connection between the ambush on his group and the attack on the Academy then-"

"It only makes sense for whatever is next to be much bigger in scale," Madam Chambers responds quietly. "Agent Connors, I do apologize, but I have to excuse myself. I appreciate your time and dedication in doing what's right. Before I go, however, I would like to offer a word of advice."

"If there is anything you take from this dear, it is that whatever comes next is going to change our world. I've already made arrangements for some of my personnel to vacate the area for their safety," Madam Chambers reveals.

"I know you are here on a mission, which is something I commend you for. But something deep inside tells me that the road ahead is not for the faint of heart."

"So, what exactly is your advice, Ma'am?"

"If you are going to stay here, then don't just do it for the LanTech Empire. Don't even do it for Agent Keyes. Do it for yourself. Look deep into yourself to see what it is you are here for and what you do from there is a simple matter."

"And that is, Madam Chambers?"

"Fight."

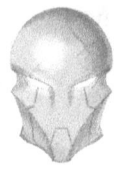

CHAPTER 3

K eenth and the others press on their journey. Though no one could fully say for certain, it was clear that an ominous feeling was present throughout Tortuga.

"I think we've spent enough time sitting still," Benjamin states. "If there is anything else worth talking about, we can do it on the way. So, if you two don't mind, let's be on our way, ladies."

"Did you just assume what my gender is? You know what, I won't even dignify that with a response," Keenth replies.

"That's actually a pretty good question," Cory lightheartedly states. "What's the plan ahead, Benjamin?"

"Benjamin? What's with the formality? My friends call me Ben, so it'll make it a lot easier on all of us—"

"No, seriously, I have a couple of things to get off my chest," Keenth exclaims.

"On second thought, never mind. Just stick with Benjamin. Anyway, we're heading towards the southeast end of Tortuga. In other words, that means we'll be out towards the end of this region. I figured within a few…Wait a second…How did you get up here in the first place, Cory?"

"Well, about that. Lord Haden brought me around the area of the Training Academy using a special ability. He gave me a scroll explaining how to do it myself to bring Keenth and I back to our temple in the forest. But between the attacks that took place, I kinda, sorta lost it…and my map."

"You mean to tell me that you had the indispensable ability to teleport from location to location at your fingertips and you lost it!" Benjamin shouts. "What kind of apprentice does that? How old are you, fourteen?"

"I am! How'd you know, Ben?"

"Benjamin! And I can't believe that I am literally surrounded by children! Don't even start, Keenth!"

"Fair enough," Keenth quietly replies. "But what's done is done. What's the plan now, Benny?"

"Well, given the amount of attacks in the western outskirts lately, it would be best for us to make our way through a major city as soon as possible," Benjamin replies after calming himself.

"Is that really the best idea? I have never been to a city before, so I would probably stick out in a bad way. Not to mention that I can't shake the feeling that you are seen as a criminal in most circles," Cory naively inquires.

"What makes you think I'm a criminal?"

"I'm pretty sure that you referred to yourself as a devil or something while fighting before, so…"

"That's different," Benjamin declares. "Look, the warriors might play by their own rules in the outskirts, but the cities around here are relatively safe."

"I may not have the best reputation among certain areas out here," Benjamin continues. "But I know that you guys will be better off in the city as opposed to out here in the sticks."

"So which city did you have in mind Ben-," Keenth began asking before flames began forming around a certain man's fist. "What did you have in mind, Benjamin?"

"It's kind of complicated. You see, most of the cities from this point are west from where we are. There's no point in going in that direction if our aim is the sage's summer camp in the southeast."

"There is, however, a large body of water ahead that separates where we'll be shortly to our destination. That is where we'll find our city"

"I didn't sign up to do an underwater detour man," Keenth blurts. "Not to mention that I can't even swim!"

"What do you mean you can't swim? Didn't you say you're from the islands?"

"Respect me!"

"Shut up," Benjamin snaps back. "Obviously what I'm getting at is that there's a bridge. Though just by looking at it, simply seeing it as a bridge would not do it any kind of justice. Keenth, you told us earlier that you are from the islands. Namely, Colonia Island, right?"

"Yeah, what about it?"

"Well," Benjamin explains to the two. "Did you know that Colonia was once a part of Hasania?"

"They say something took place many years ago that was powerful enough to reshape Hasania forever. Don't you get it? Colonia and its neighboring islands are what's left of the region."

"Are you serious?"

"Of course. There may be people in the world with abilities beyond your imagination, but no one could make the content whole again. Instead, the people started building a massive bridge over time. As the years passed, they expanded to a massive city-like structure over the ocean."

"So, what's the name of this city?" Cory asks.

"Bridge, Cory. Be it as it may, there are generations worth of pride behind what began as the means to rebuild what was lost many, many years ago. So, yeah, it is a bridge and it's known as the Prospear Bridge. That, my friends, is our destination."

*

Back in the Intel Detachment, investigating the Training Academy, Agent Giles is on a remote call to Agent Connors' office.

Feeling the need to speak to someone about the meeting that took place with Madam Chambers, Agent Connors finds herself somewhat conflicted about how to move forward.

"Ah, I see," Agent Giles assesses. "I appreciate you taking the time to tell me and all, but where exactly do I come in with this?"

"I don't know; maybe because I know you wouldn't answer unless I said it was urgent," Agent Connors responds.

"Or maybe because I know better than to discuss something like this over an unsecured line. That and I figure that the, I don't know, Senior Intel Specialist should know as much as well?"

"They'll never find your body, Ro."

"Sure, okay. Anyway, based on what you told me, I believe that there is reason to be concerned about a pending attack on the horizon. If we really have a target on our backs, then there really aren't too many other places that are in danger in Tortuga."

"Well, we have other facilities scattered throughout Hasania, but something tells me they would not be worth attacking. Of course, there is our LanTech Headquarters in the southern region of Sadeena, but I doubt anyone would be foolish enough to attack that stronghold."

"Hell, I'm an Agent, and I don't even like going there unless I have to. Regardless, we need to take a step back and reevaluate the facts at hand."

"You're right, my friend. Speaking of which, where are we at with reviewing the information regarding the Training Academy?"

"Ah, well, seeing how he brought it up, I had Agent Fallon take the lead on that. I imagine he should have something for us within the next couple of days."

"Truth be told, we don't have a couple of days. We don't exactly have time at our disposal. If he didn't complete that task, then why did you think to grant him personal leave?"

"Personal leave? What are you talking about?" a confused Agent Giles replies.

"What, seriously? I received your message where you said you would be granting him a few days of personal leave. Here, you can take a look yourself."

Agent Giles remains silent as he reads the message forwarded from Agent Connors. He knew for a fact that this was his first time seeing it, but since it was an encrypted message, it would appear otherwise.

"Strange, this is the first that I have heard of this. To send this kind of message would require my credentials, pin number..."

"...I know, Giles, I know. But this leads to the obvious question: Where is Agent Fallon?"

*

"Hey, can we grab some postcards while we're here," Keenth requests. "I can't wait 'til my friends get a load of this place."

"For the seventh time, no! Besides, I doubt you even have any friends," Benjamin scorns. "We've only been here for a few hours and you're already getting on my nerves."

It took little over a day, but the trio finally made it to their designated destination. As Keenth and Benjamin continued to go back and forth, Cory was at a loss for words at the structure that is the Prospear Bridge.

The liveliness of the bridge was unmistakable–between its people, culture, and overall spirit, the young girl found herself humble to experience it all firsthand.

"Hey. guys, I was thinking about something. After we reach Lord Haden, what happens from there?"

"Hmm? Isn't he your boss? I figured you would have more answers when it comes to that," Benjamin responds. "While I'm down there, there are a few things that I would like to ask him myself."

"Seriously, Benjamin? What kind of questions do you have?"

"Don't worry about it. I'll bring it up to the old man when the time comes," Benjamin answers. "That reminds me, what makes this Haden guy such a big deal?" Keenth interjects. "What exactly makes him so important around here?"

"Well, for one, that's Lord Haden," Cory states, correcting Keenth. "And, also, he is the Sage of Hatre. Not that my own abilities are much to speak of, but he is many times more powerful than you could imagine."

"Sage of Hatre?"

"What exactly did they teach you around here anyway?" Benjamin chimes in. "Hatre are more or less Earth-based abilities. There are tons out there that I don't care to remember, mainly because of being on the receiving end of them."

"He's right. You've already come into contact with at least one person using some Hatre-based abilities. Remember Vera? I recognized some of her techniques, though it should be obvious that her tactics would not be as refined as those under the guidance of Lord Haden," Cory states.

"Whoa, are you serious? I really can't wait to meet Ha—, I mean, Lord Haden then. Do you think he can teach me a few moves?" Keenth asks, being laughed off by Benjamin.

"Ha! If only things were that simple. Using Hatre, or any elemental-based abilities for that matter, involves a lot more than just being taught. There are different factors like experience, lineage, physical and spiritual capability," Benjamin explains.

"I'm sure there's a reason why the three of us are making the journey down there, but showing you how to throw rocks at people probably isn't one of them."

"Hey now! We do way more than throw rocks, you know!"

"Don't make me laugh! I've already shown you two firsthand that Efir abilities stand well above the others!"

"Unless there's a small rain shower in the area!"

"Take that back, you little brat!"

"Not before you apologize, you...filthy man!"

"Can I grab some postcards while you two are at it? It'll only take a—"Keenth was silenced by their piercing glares.

It was around that time he felt nostalgia. Even though these three were still in the beginning of their adventure, there was a true sense of belonging among them.

"Say, Cory, going back to what you asked," Keenth speaks up. "About the whole, you know, what happens next thing. I'm really not sure what Lord Haden has in mind, but once the smoke clears, I see myself going back home to Colonia."

"Really? Why is that?" Cory asks.

"I mean, do I really need a sign bigger than the Academy being attacked to tell me to make changes."

"Ah, I see where you are coming from, Keenth. I don't know Lord Haden's plan either, but I believe it will be for the best," Cory assures.

"I mean, look where it has taken us so far. I never would have thought to be on an adventure like this, exploring places and meeting you two along the way. I don't know about you guys, but I really appreciate the opportunity!"

"You and me both," Keenth exclaims. "When it's all said and done, I wouldn't mind hanging out with you some more. There is more of Tortuga that I want to see and since we're being honest, I like to think I'm in pretty good company."

"I agree! How about you, Benjamin?"

Even though Benjamin initially had a puzzled expression on his face, he couldn't help, but be affected by Cory's positive spirit.

"Sure, fine. You guys can count me in too."

"Well, my only condition is that you two step it up. I'll be damned if I'm the only one putting all the work in!"

"Oh, please! I'm confident in saying that I'm probably one of the best swordsmen that the world has ever seen! I'm sure I'll do just fine, thank you very much," Keenth replies.

"Yeah, sure. In case you didn't notice, this isn't exactly the island life anymore. This is the real deal—"

Before Benjamin could finish, a massive explosion erupts from behind the group. Even though it was from miles away, the shockwave is enough to knock the trio down.

In the moments that followed, Keenth finds himself trying to regain his composure.

The attack left ominous clouds of smoke in its wake that Keenth was all too familiar with. But unlike the ones that were created by Benjamin in the forest, they were from explosions similar to the attack on the Training Academy.

Keenth picks himself up and, after helping Cory on her feet, he begins walking toward the explosion against his better judgment. Before he could move any further, Benjamin chastises him.

"It should not take me spelling this out for you, but now is not the time to be playing hero!"

"Who said anything about playing? This is the same thing that happened at my Academy, so I know what I'm up against here!"

"Which is exactly why you two need to get the hell out of here! Listen to me, you're not using your head. Rushing over there is the last thing you should be doing. Going there isn't going to undo what they did, Keenth!"

"But it will stop them from doing this again. Look. I may not have much to bring to the table, but there are other people on this bridge. Innocent people who are going through what I barely came out of. The fact that I'm here has to be for a reason and I've gotta do whatever I can right now to. I just can't look the other way, Ben."

Benjamin nods before laying out the plan. Realizing the importance of reaching the sage, he advises Cory to accompany Keenth to continue onward, while Benjamin draws the attention of the attackers towards himself.

"Hey, I know we're all clear that if things get out of hand, Cory and I are here to help the others on the bridge too," Keenth said before moving forward. "But what happens if the two of us aren't enough?"

"Then they go through me," Benjamin exclaims as he rushes directly towards danger. Discarding his cloak, his right arm is shrouded in mighty powerful flames which he unleashes as a massive Efir-based flamethrower in an amazing display.

Benjamin watches intently as several figures emerge through the flames. One by one, each opponent appeared, at least fifteen by his count.

Whether it was their tattered military fatigues or the emotionless expressions on their battle-worn masks, the only feeling coursing throughout Benjamin's body was despair.

Even though he is a seasoned warrior in his own right, it was as if this was the first time that he was up against the embodiment of death itself.

Not to let himself become intimidated, Benjamin questions his opponents' intentions as a means to buy the others time to escape the area.

"Don't take it the wrong way, but you all seem a bit too old to be playing dress up. That and it wouldn't hurt if you guys considered wearing name tags or something. After all, I like to know the names of those I beat beyond recognition."

"No need for formalities, Benjamin Palorro, Son of Maroso," a figure draped in chainmail responds. "While your power is formidable when compared to the rest in this region, I'm afraid you'll find that our methods are able to deal with you."

"Oh, is that a fact? Well, thanks for clearing my suspicions of you not being from around here. It is one thing for me not to recognize you, but that's not enough. Were you the ones behind the attack on the Training Academy?" "Among others, yes. Strange. ..I did not take you for the sentimental type, Mr. Palorro. I assumed you would be supportive of any action, no matter the means, that would lead towards the demise of the LanTech Empire. After all, they were the same group that cast a shadow over Hasania. It all but left the legacy of—"

"Yup, just another nobody."

"I beg your pardon, young warrior?"

"Nothing. It's just that if you won't bother telling me who you are, then I'm going to treat you like the nameless trash that you are," Benjamin responds, while walking towards the hooded figure.

And don't think I'll give you the satisfaction of striking a nerve: I could care less about your problems with LanTech or your reasoning behind your actions. And while it's true my people were known for protecting Hasania, you'll find I am not nearly as forgiving!"

With the hooded figure in an unassuming stance, Benjamin saw an opportunity to attack his opponent. Placing his right arm forward, Benjamin unleashed a blazing attack that was just short of reaching his target.

Confused by this, he soon realizes that a loyal subordinate jumped in harm's way to prevent Benjamin from emerging victorious.

"You seem surprised. There are ideals in this world that are bigger than you could ever hope to comprehend. Actions that have been a very long time in the making," the figure explains.

"You are among those who are fortunate enough to see the world as we know it come to an end. This is the Age of the Metallic Siege. You asked for my name, yes? You may refer to me as Varun, the Prophet—the prophet of your demise."

Before Benjamin could react, the scorched mercenary leaped from the ground and began strangling him. Trying to pull the death grip from his neck was to no avail, so Benjamin released a fireball at close range. To his shock, his adversary was completely unfazed.

"I commend you for committing to your beliefs until the end,"

Varun proclaimed. "But I'm afraid leaving you alive would, in turn, tarnish our beliefs. We will change the world, child. And that includes finishing what we started at that forsaken Academy."

Raising Benjamin up with his right arm, the mercenary summons a blade with his free hand. In the blink of an eye, the mercenary found their vision obscured by Benjamin's cloak of all things.

Releasing Benjamin to assess the situation, the foe is immediately ambushed. This strike proved to be powerful enough to be knock back Varun and the other mercenaries. Catching his breath, Benjamin is shocked at who decided to join the fray.

"Keenth!"

"The one and only! Did you miss me, handsome?"

"What are you doing here? The plan was for you to get out of here! Can't you see this isn't a game?"

"Sure, but I don't remember you getting killed being something we agreed on," Keenth retorts. "Let's just say I had a change of heart–we'll just have to iron out the details some other time."

"What makes you think being here will make much of a difference," Benjamin smirks. "You know that you can't save the world on your own, right?"

"Well, it's a good thing that he's not alone," Cory responds.

Emerging with a handful of warriors, Cory explains that others joined the cause after seeing Benjamin selflessly putting himself in harm's way. This act of unity proved that Varun was wrong about the people of Hasania.

"Do you really think a group of low-level rebels will make a difference here?" Varun asks. "I believe I said that you'll find our methods more than capable of dealing with you. Allow me to erase any doubts from your feeble minds."

A hulking mercenary emerged from behind Varun, kicking their fallen comrade with great might towards Keenth and the others. Varun raised his right hand in the air and made it a fist, causing the foe to explode.

"So that's how you did it," Keenth shouts. "That's how you attacked us at the Academy! It's time that you pay for that!"

"Why waste your time mourning for the fallen when you will soon be among them?" Varun responds. "You might not have had the opportunity to catch up with Mr. Palorro, but I made our intentions of finishing what we started very clear."

Realizing the meaning of his words, Keenth came to the shocking realization that he was their target all along. Guilt-ridden, Keenth asked Benjamin if this was the reason why he was so adamant in getting Keenth out of the immediate area.

Without directly responding, Benjamin opted to make things clear with Varun.

"You'll find that the warriors that stand here will be enough to handle your worst. The only thing that today will be remembered for is a false prophet and his minions being bested by the proudest that Hasania has to offer," Benjamin proclaims.

Benjamin's words rallied the others to prepare for battle. Immediately, the warriors found themselves swarmed by dozens of more mercenaries. Despite only having about ten warriors among them, they courageously stood ready to defy the odds.

With his arm still in the air, Varun waved it down, signaling the mercenaries to attack. Noticing this, Benjamin led the allies to do the same. He, Cory, and Keenth charged towards Varun, while striking down any and all opposition on their path.

This task proved to be more difficult than originally intended once they realized the mercenaries greatly varied in size, scope, and skill. A brute lunged at Keenth, only for his two known allies to defend him, thwarting the attack.

Through the chaos, Benjamin and Cory were proud at Keenth's resolve, which, in turn, motivated them to push even harder. Despite all of this, it seemed as though their efforts were not enough against the unrelenting assault.

Varun causes the fallen mercenaries to explode across the battlefield. What made matters worse is that he could do the same for mercenaries still actively engaged in combat. Enraged, Keenth and Benjamin blitz toward Varun, only for a group of opponents to surround them.

"Clearly, it was enough to rally the others among you and, for that, you have my respect. With that taken into consideration, it makes it all the clearer to eliminate the most powerful among you here and now."

"If that's how you feel, then just leave Benjamin out of this!"

"This really isn't the time or place, Keenth," Benjamin shouts. "Besides, it's obvious that he was talking about me!"

As the two continued to argue, they slowly realized that Varun raised his fist in the air. Cory called out her allies' names the explosions go off before they could even react.

Once the smoke cleared, Cory noticed a large wall of ice protecting Keenth and Benjamin. The source of this came from a young woman standing on one of the nearby arches.

Though a surprise to most on the bridge, Keenth vaguely recognized the person from a distance. Calling her Susan, his thanks are quickly brushed aside.

"Feel free to get my name right and show your thanks if we survive this," Beth replies.

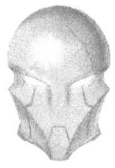

CHAPTER 4

"Ayo, Icebox! As much as I appreciate the hand, don't even think about stealing my thunder," Benjamin states.

"But I thought using fire was your thing," Keenth retorts.

"It's called Efir, you fool! You know what I mean! Besides, I have this under control and the last thing I need is any more chefs in the kitchen."

"…Yeah, great. Anyway, my name's Beth. Beth Masterson, Executive Assistant of the Tortugan High Council. I'm here since I owe you one."

Keenth could barely hide his confusion at Beth's words as she approached them. While he was somewhat familiar with the light blue Tortugan Service Uniform, it was her above average height that especially sparked his interest.

With her dark-brown hair gracefully flowing in the wind, and—

"Uh, hello? Why are you staring at my eyes like that? Don't be a creep."

"I'm trying to figure out what color your eyes are, Susan!"

"Hazel! More importantly call me Susan instead of Beth again and I'll make an example out of you that you won't soon forget. Are we good?"

"We're good. Shoot, you can even say I see you eye to hazel eye—"

Cory swatted the back of Keenth's head before he could embarrass himself any further. After formally introducing herself, Cory asked Beth to elaborate on what she said earlier.

"Right. A couple of my people were in the area when the attack began. Fortunately, they were able to board a large airship to get away from the chaos. They didn't get anyone's names, but they were able to describe two particular standouts leading the way."

"Let me guess: A warrior and a mage," Keenth confidently stated.

"More like a kid in a wizard's robe and some sword-wielding jackass."

"Name-calling is totally uncalled for. And the joke's on them since Cory doesn't even use a swo—go on."

"Anyway, as I was rushing to the bridge, all I thought to myself was that it should have been me there. I guess what I'm trying to say is that your efforts have not gone unnoticed. I don't know what their reasoning is behind the attack, but allow me to repay my debt to you guys," Beth assures.

"Hey, that's what I like to hear! Welcome to the party," Benjamin replies. "You couldn't have come at a better time. Truth be told, the guys fighting alongside us are fatigued, so we can't keep this up for too much longer."

"What do you suggest we do? I pushed myself to get here as soon as possible, but I still have enough in my tank to put these low lives in their place."

"Let's just say that babysitting Keenth has been particularly draining, so I'm not exactly at a hundred percent either. These guys aren't tough on their own, but fighting them off again and again is definitely taking its toll."

"I figured as much. Even when surrounded by pawns, you still have to keep your eye on their king."

"Well, that's a lot easier said than done. Even if we have the perfect opening, his crew keeps that Varun guy untouchable. Just take a look, we haven't even been able to scratch him."

"Maybe I could help with that," Cory interjects. "It was hard to figure it out earlier, but I think I understand their attack patterns. "I have a solution, though it isn't exactly a practical one."

"We're all ears, Cory. What's the plan?"

"Okay, so up until now, I haven't had the chance to properly gather Hatre energy. It won't be much, but I can give you and Keenth the opening needed to keep the focus on guys."

"Hmm, I think we can work with that. By now, I'm sure they have a pretty good handle on some of my Efir techniques, so if you see an opening, you strike that bastard down, Keenth!"

"You don't have to tell me twice! How about you, Beth? What are you going to do?" a fired-up Keenth asks.

"It'll take a bit to get ready, but I think the best technique to use is one I like to call Gelida. One touch from me, and he'll be frozen in an instant," Beth reveals.

"The only catch is preparing this leaves me open for attack. So, if there's anything I ask, it's that you boys don't let me down."

"Fair enough! You can count on us! After all, difficult takes a day, impossible takes—"

Keenth is interrupted by Cory's Hatre-Crown ability that caused

Realizing the stones were forming in sporadic bursts, Benjamin knew that this was their opportunity to catch their opponents by surprise. Keenth, on the other hand, would hopefully come to the same conclusion as well.

"Come on, Cory! A little heads up would be nice! I can barely dodge these—Gah!"

While Keenth was *adjusting*, Benjamin rejoined the fray, equipped with two silver chakrams hidden in his sash.

Looking to conserve his energy and mix things up with his opponents, he engulfed these weapons with Efir flames to enhance his strikes.

"And here I figured the least a Sage Apprentice attack would be is something worth mentioning," Varun taunts. "I pray you insects would muster a final resistance worth remembering."

"That's the plan. Hope you like the view!"

Confused by Cory's words, Varun finds himself rising on a platform created by her Hatre. Stone spears were created to separate him from the rest of the foes. Despite this, Varun only saw this as delaying the inevitable.

"Surely, you didn't think this would be enough to slow me down, child. I commend your efforts, but I assure you that you all are fated to receive an agonizing execution by my hand."

"Well, if that's what you have in mind, then consider this your guillotine!"

Before Varun could react to the voice from above him, Benjamin combined his weapons to release a monstrous flame shaped as an angled blade.

This attack was powerful enough to not only destroy Cory's solid stone pillar, but incapacitate the surrounding enemies as well.

Having exhausted his remaining energy, Benjamin fell from the sky and was completely worn out. Despite a direct hit from such a devastating move, Varun emerged from the flames, albeit critically harmed.

Looking to destroy Benjamin with a critical blow, Varun was astonished to find himself unable to move.

"What is this?"

"It's the end of the line, you monster. Defeat at the hands of those you've underestimated," Beth says while firmly gripping her opponent's shoulder. "May your corpse shatter with everything you stand for!"

"Damn you!"

Beth releases a massive discharge that encased the entire surrounding area in ice. Benjamin realizes that his flames diminish as a frozen haze hauntingly encompassed them.

Following a brief moment of silence, he gave his newfound ally her due praise.

"You did it. You really did it. So much for needing us to buy you time, Icebox."

"I lied, well, sort of. To use Gelida at its full potential, I need a decent amount of prep time. But if you factor in the water below us and that he was intent on killing you…Well, I think you can figure out the rest," Beth replies as she catches her breath.

"It looks to me like you pushed yourself to make up for lost time… It really says a lot about you," Benjamin replies. "Thank you for making that risk for me, for us. I'm just about spent myself, so I know where you are coming from."

"Sure thing, don't mention it. I have allies that should be here shortly to—"

Beth was unable to finish speaking due to being impaled through the stomach by a broken spear. Falling to the ground, she turned around to see Varun gazing down on her.

Questioning how he could possibly survive her attack, Varun rebuked the notion of being measured by mere human standards.

"Let it be known that compassion for the fool over there is what led to your death, woman. Had you properly executed your strategy, your efforts might have proven slightly more successful," Varun announces as he raised his spear over Beth's head.

Grabbing Varun's wrist, Beth immobilizes her opponent when his guard was down. Despite finding that he truly could not move, he mused at the fact that Beth and the others still continued to exhaust their efforts in vain.

"It will only be a moment before I free myself yet again. It is obvious that you are all out of options. Do you really think this will change your fates?"

"Y-you must have missed the part when I said you underestimate us...NOW!"

At that moment, Cory rescues Beth out of Varun's reach. Before he could ready an attack on the two, Keenth immediately swings down on the opponent, severing Varun's arm in the process.

"That...was for my Academy! As for what you did to Beth and everyone else that you've hurt and I'm just getting started."

"Ah, I see. So, your plan all along was to disarm me so that I couldn't utilize my group...Such guerilla tactics...Very impressive," Varun says as he was unable to rise from the ground. "Despite being inferior to me, the four of you stand triumphant..."

"Say what you want, but you're finished. It's all over," Keenth states as he readies his stance. Now more than ever, Keenth felt motivated to truly avenge the fallen from the Academy, as well as ensure the efforts of Beth and the others were fully realized.

"What a shame...Here I thought we were able to comprehend one another," Varun says as he rises before Keenth. His young opponent attempts to deliver the finishing blow, but Varun sends Keenth flying back several feet, only to be stopped by one of Beth's frozen formations.

"While you have earned some of my respect, that does not change the fact your light will be consumed by darkness. As will the rest of Hasania."

These were Varun's final words as he finally collapsed, causing the surrounding area to shake violently.

Keenth and the others regrouped only to realize that Varun's defeat had caused the remainder of his mercenaries to begin emitting destructive energy, which would soon explode throughout Prospear Bridge.

This was their objective all along: To destroy a symbol of hope and unity throughout the region. Keenth drops to his knees when he realizes that Varun might have been right in saying that they could not change fate.

"Keenth...Keenth! Now's not the time to give up," Benjamin shouts as he helps him to his feet. "We didn't make it this far just to lose now..."

"He's right," Beth supports. "After all, I refuse to believe that this is how our story ends."

"What can we do? There's way too many of them about to go off and there's not enough time to leave the area," Keenth says, trying to get himself together.

"Well, that's the thing. It's less of a goal that deals with us and more of one that deals with you," Cory says approaching Keenth.

"As despicable as our enemy was, I agree with him when it comes to fate. That said, I feel that it's part of our fate to get you out of here safely."

"What the hell are you talking about? There's no way we aren't leaving together! I've been down this road before and I refuse to let it ever happen again."

"While we appreciate the thought, you have to be realistic. I'm barely able to stand and that's only thanks to Cory healing what she could with the little strength she has left," Beth says, shattered pieces of ice covering her wound. "I'm only deadweight at this point. Don't let me or any of us slow you down…"

Keenth was speechless, but the expression on his face spoke volumes. Seeing how selfless his allies were in the face of impending doom caused him to feel an abundance of emotions.

His eyes began to well with tears as his comrades smiled at him in reassurance. Before he could respond, Keenth swiftly fell out of consciousness. Beth and Cory began to speak about this, but Benjamin insisted this was for the best.

"What are you giving me that look for? I'm pretty sure that the kid was starting to cry and we don't have a lot of time left," Benjamin says as he eases Keenth down.

"Besides, I'm sure he won't let us down. At least, I hope he won't."

"I would never take you as someone who banked on hope," Cory teases.

"Yeah, yeah. More importantly, are you sure that you're up for this? There's really no turning back from here."

"Thank you, Benjamin, but I've already made my decision. Lord Haden entrusted me with protecting Keenth from malicious forces on his journey and I have done my best to fulfill that," Cory carries on, while holding back tears.

"I j-just hope that if we don't make it alive, that at least, he'll remember me..."

"Of course, he will. I'm sure of it, Cory. Come on, now's the time. Take my hand. You oughta join in too, Beth. I could use all the help that I can get."

Even though she was initially confused, Beth joined Benjamin and Cory to form a triangle around Keenth.

Benjamin wasn't properly trained using teleportation abilities, but he knew enough to attempt to send Keenth out of the area.

With their eyes closed, they put their remaining efforts in saving the young man.

"Alright, I need you guys to focus your Auraen to align with mine for this. We only have one shot, but we're not sending him to Lord Haden. I can only teleport someone to a place that I've been to before. But by trying to send him to where I have in mind, I know he will be in good hands soon."

"Well, Benjamin, I'm not sure what you're talking about, but it's now or never," Beth says, sensing that they only had a few moments left.

"Call me, Ben. Even though I feel a certain way about how it ended, I wouldn't have met up with you three otherwise. It's been real, guys! Alright, here goes nothing!"

Focusing the last of their power on Keenth, the four are surrounded by a soft white light.

"Stay alive, Keenth. We won't be too far behind...And that's a promise..."

*

Aya speeds on her motorcycle, only to be stopped in her tracks at the sight of a bright blue glow engulfing the Prospear Bridge from a distance.

She slowly removes her helmet to observe this unnatural phenomenon.

Dropping her phone with Madam Chambers on the line, her inaudible reaction gradually became a piercing scream of sorrow and despair.

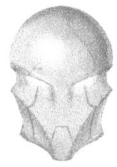

CHAPTER 5

"6-0406, Agent Jennifer Connors reporting."

"At ease, Agent Connors. I am Director Byron Alteme, and I will be overseeing this special hearing that you have requested. Also in attendance are elite Agents, Laurent Masterson and Elise Van, along with members of the Executive Council," Director Alteme states from his podium.

"Though this special hearing was made at your request, please note that members of the Executive Council and myself can conclude this hearing at any time. Do you understand, Agent Connors?"

"Yes, Sir," Agent Connors replied before she sat. "Respectfully, requesting to provide my opening statement."

Taking place just days after the attack on the Prospear Bridge, the atmosphere of the special hearing was tense.

Several members of the Executive Council speak among themselves before signaling Agent Connors to proceed.

"Greetings to the Executive Director, my elite Agents, and members of the council. Thank you for granting a special hearing in regards to

Agent Keyes' investigation. As the leading Agent of the investigation, I am respectfully requesting additional manpower and resources in order to conduct this properly."

"We granted what you initially requested and you could not accomplish things then. What benefit would come from entertaining your request, Ms. Connors? How would things be any different now?" one of the councilmen asks.

"Given the recent attacks on the Training Academy and the Prospear Bridge, we have reason to believe that they are connected to the Keyes Investigation. Given the scale of these incidences, this warrants additional support. Support, as you know, that would require to be granted by the Executive Council," Agent Connors responds.

"You didn't answer his question, so allow me to rephrase, Ms. Connors. What makes you think that you are in any position to support this investigation any more than you already have with additional funds?" another councilman bluntly states.

Knowing that the members of the Executive Council were attempting to unnerve her, Agent Connors was mindful not to let their behavior get the better of her. Instead, she opted to provide projections on where the investigation would go.

"Let me make this as clear as possible, Agent Connors. The handling of the Keyes Investigation has been a failure in the eyes of the Executive Council and, frankly, the world over," Director Alteme states, while those in attendance collectively agree with murmurs.

"The stagnant nature of this investigation was in no way beneficial to the already apprehensive perception of the LanTech Empire. So, for you to request this hearing in an attempt to fruitlessly pour even more resources into this is absolutely arrogant on your part."

"I'm sorry, but arrogant? Do you consider spearheading an

investigation on the murder of a veteran Agent to be arrogant? Maybe reports and statements regarding all of this are not enough to justify your opinion on how crucial this operation is so I will say it like this," Agent Connors replies, staring directly at Director Alteme.

"Agent Keyes was just the beginning. If individuals could attack him, knowing the ramifications that would follow, what's to say that they would not attack the Training Academy as well? Or a goddamn bridge halfway to hell like they did with Prospear? If we don't get to the root of this, there is no telling how dark things will get."

"And would that be such a problem, Agent Connors? Would that be such a hindrance for you and your fellow Agents?" Director Alteme counters. "Perhaps the real root of the issue is that there are those in the world who felt comfortable enough to strike the 'Invincible Empire' in the first place."

"I'm not sure what you are implying, but I'll have you know that I have faithfully served as an Agent for years without the need to prove my status by blind force. That was a principle passed on to me by the late Agent Keyes and I'll be damned if that stops anytime soon."

"If principles like those are what he stood by, it is no small wonder that he's not standing here to speak for himself right now, is it?" Director Alteme replies.

"Understand this," Director Alteme continues. "Well before this investigation, the Executive Council has expressed its thoughts on how complacent certain personnel among the LanTech Empire have become over the years. It was only a matter of time before others took the opportunity to turn the tide."

"Battles and wars take place in Hasania and the rest of the world, we all know that to be true. LanTech has served as a means of balancing the order. To suggest that we play the roles of judge, jury, and executioner is not balance–it is tyranny," Agent Connors replies.

"The fact that we are even entertaining this hearing goes to show how far this movement has fallen, Connors. Do you really think the rest of the world is taking a pause while we have this little gathering? No, this will not do. It will not do at all."

"Enough of this! Agent Connors, let it be known that you have officially been relieved as the leading Agent in charge of the Keyes Investigation, effective immediately. From here, you will return to your post under Elite Agent Masterson in terms of generating a dominant presence throughout the northwestern region of Cordela."

"Director! What is there to gain from this? We have come too far with this investigation just to let it go to the wayside."

"Yes, but the Keyes Investigation isn't coming to a close," Director Alteme replies.

"56-0409, Agent James Fallon reporting."

"Wait, Fallon? Fallon?? What the hell is going on here?!" Agent Connors questions as the young man comes forward. "Is this some kind of joke? Explain yourself!"

"There isn't anything to explain. At least not to you, Agent Connors. This decision is out of my hands," Agent Fallon responds.

"The data that I've gathered throughout the investigation was falling on deaf ears. Knowing how important all of this is, I forwarded that information up the chain. From there, the Executive Council made their determination that—"

"So, you think you can bypass me just to get your point across and there won't be any consequences? You have a lot of things coming to you!"

"That's enough. From all of you," Agent Masterson says. "It seems as though the council made their decision long before you even requested this hearing, Agent Connors."

"Then it is settled," Director Alteme, says motioning for the hearing to reach its conclusion. "Be sure to turn over any and all classified materials relating to the Keyes Investigation to Agent Fallon before departing for Cordela, Agent Connors."

"Not just yet," Agent Masterson adds. "While I acknowledge the Executive Council's decision with changes regarding the Keyes Investigation, I cannot in good faith allow such a junior Agent to single-handedly take the reins."

"Then what do you suggest, Masterson?"

"Bring in Agent Giles as a Senior Advisor to the Keyes Investigation. Given his familiarity with the case and his standing as an Agent, it would be in the best interest of everyone moving forward. Namely, Command Officer Lansient, who suggested Agent Giles in case the changes regarding the investigation were to take place."

"So, your Commander anticipated such. Interesting...Very well, we'll allow it. With that, this hearing has come to a close," Director Alteme states as the Executive Council looms from a distance.

Solemnly nodding to Agent Masterson and having given so much towards the investigation, Agent Connors collects herself before acknowledging the changes that were well beyond her control.

"May your actions reflect the interests of the LanTech Empire going forward. If the recent events have told us anything, it is that your adversaries will not hesitate to destroy you and everything you stand for. Be sure to enforce that same sentiment," Director Alteme orders.

"Right...By any means," Agent Fallon thinks to himself.

*

That same morning, Aya arrives at the Tortugan capital at Madam Chambers' request. Echoing what was said at the special hearing, the people were growing restless of the recent attacks. Change, whether good or bad, was definitely on the horizon.

"Ma'am, I take it you arranged this meeting so I wouldn't just barge in unannounced," Aya drily states. "Did you really think making me take a couple days of leave would be enough for things to cool things over?"

"Aya, you don't have nearly even enough days on the books to ever calm yourself down," Madam Chambers replies. "These last few days were more disturbing for me than anyone else. I just needed some time to gather my thoughts. Though I hate to say it, a few days just weren't enough, given the circumstances."

"I understand, Ma'am. So, what do we do from here," Aya says as she sits down. "Something, well, anything, is better than just waiting for the next attack to happen."

"As you know, I've tried to be as transparent as I could as your leader and mentor throughout the years, but I do believe this is the first time I have no clear direction."

"When I entered the position as the Tortuga High Council, it was a means to help unify us," Madam Chambers continues. "While there have been highs and lows along the way, it was always proven time and time again that we were on a positive path. But it seems that all of that changed."

"If you're blaming yourself for some reason, then please stop right there," Aya replies. "Everything we stand for has been a pillar for Tortuga and beyond. If we start giving up hope when Tortuga needs us, then we'll only have ourselves to blame, when all is said and done."

"Hmm. Who would've thought young Ayanna would be the one

giving wisdom to an old relic like myself? That's the spirit, alright. Thank you," Madam Chambers warmly states. "We'll get through this. The fire of hope is still smoldering yet."

"As long as you at least try to simply call me Aya, then consider me in. We may not have a lot of personnel and resources at the moment, but if my time here has taught me anything, we will definitely make do with what we have."

"Absolutely, Aya. Speaking of which, I have some news about Elizabeth."

"Really?? What kind of news? How is she doing?"

"Well. Elizabeth, I'm sorry, Beth is gradually recovering from her injuries. We are definitely grateful, considering many others on the bridge did not make it out alive."

"Beth. She would be too stubborn to let a freaking terror attack keep her down," a relieved Aya responds. "I really can't say I'm surprised that she's okay."

"If I didn't know any better, it sounds like you expected me to kick the bucket!"

"Beth!"

"The one and only," Beth responds from Madam Chambers' phone. "Since I couldn't be there in person, I asked if I could be placed on speaker. Had I known you would be blabbing away, then I probably would have—"

"You idiot," Aya quietly responds, holding back tears. "You stupid, idiot."

"Yeah, yeah. Missed you too, Aya. We can catch up later, but have we heard from our personnel in the area? Are they okay?"

"Oh! Yes, their airship was able to take off. Word has it that some loud mouth brat and a few others were fending off attackers so that people could escape," Aya replies. "I thought it was a joke at first, but after hearing that—"

"They were saved by some idiot with a sword." Beth quietly laughs to herself. "He has a name...His name is Keenth. A bit rough around the edges, but the kid has heart."

"Stop the press: Beth actually made a friend? Despite the circumstances, I am truly speechless at the thought," Madam Chambers jokingly interjects. "All things considered; it looks like there was some good to come out of this as well."

"It was one hell of a ride alright. Something that I won't forget anytime soon," Beth replies.

"There were dozens of those stone-faced attackers. And this guy named Ben with flames. Oh, and Cory! How could I forget Cory? She saved my life! Well, technically, it was a group effort, so it doesn't really—"

"It sounds like there's a lot we've got to talk about. Maybe over some drinks once you are back on your feet," Aya suggests. "You'd be paying, of course. Don't expect any sympathy from me, young lady."

"Don't you dare young lady me, Aya! I'll have you know that you still have tabs from months ago that you tried passing on me. Besides, everyone knows that I—"

Beth begins to violently cough. Despite saying that she was fine, her nurses then insist that she rests and Madam Chambers agrees. Aya quietly gathers her thoughts before leaving the room.

"What are you going to do, Aya? What is your plan moving forward?" Madam Chambers calls out.

"These bastards...If they had their way, my best friend wouldn't be alive. Even though she barely survived, she's sitting there coughing up her own blood. I won't rest until I see that the ones behind this are destroyed. By any means necessary, Ma'am…"

*

Meanwhile, the sun shines brightly on a man along the southeastern coast of Tortuga. Despite days passing since the Prospear incident took place, the surrounding area was still understandably in shambles.

Officials of this region had the safety of its people in mind by declaring a state of emergency. Still, that didn't stop this individual from moving along.

"Hey! I know you can hear me! How could you ignore someone that's drowning?"

"You say that, but you are obviously floating just fine! How about you start by giving your name," an old fisherman replies from his small boat.

"You've gotta be…You know what, fine, whatever. Roland! My name is Roland! Now would you please lend a brother a hand already," Roland states as he struggles to stay afloat.

The fisherman grumpily helps Roland to safety. Roland attempts to help himself to a loaf of bread, but is stopped when the fisherman threatens to skin him alive. Roland, now shackled, decides to break the tension with some small talk.

"Thanks again for saving me and not skinning me alive. Anyway, I really appreciate it. I'll be sure to pay you as soon as I get to land," Roland states as his stomach growls.

"Don't bother. Your money's no good to me," the fisherman replies. "Besides, I have no intentions of bringing you back to where I stay."

"With all due respect, if that's your way of saying you are going to kill me, then you know what? I'm not even mad," Roland shrugs. "If that's the case, I'm willing to bet that it beats drowning."

"Even though I may end up regretting it, I'm just going to drop you off once I finish my rounds here. I don't want to waste any time in these waters, so I hope you can understand me being blunt about things."

"I'm more of a paper kind of guy, but, sure, I'm picking up what you're putting down. While you are being uncharacteristically decent, do you mind sharing your name?" Roland asks.

"Weiss. Craig Weiss. Considering that I'm a fisherman and that you are on my boat, feel free to call me Skipper Weiss," he explains. "What brings you around these parts, Roland? You're not one of those rebel punks, are you?"

"Clutch my pearls! I take offense to that good, Sir," Roland says with his hand on his chest. "I'm a pretty well-known journalist. I'm sure you've heard of me."

"..."

"Well, okay, maybe not the most well-known one," Roland grunts.

"I wasn't big enough to get involved covering the attack on the Academy. I had no luck when I reached out for statements and it didn't help that they sealed off the area. I figured I could put together something short and sweet on the Prospear Bridge in the meantime and..."

"I see," Weiss responded. "Regardless of what got you there, you should be grateful that you made it out alive. Once I got wind of what happened, I made my way up here. It's been days and I was afraid that I wouldn't find anyone alive, but here you are."

"That's pretty noble of you, Skip. Though I think you should head back home as soon as you can," Roland states. "Sure, I'm not a threat but the way things have been going lately, I think you would be better off getting somewhere safe."

"I'm fifty-six years old, young buck. I'm stuck in my ways and if there's one thing for sure, I'll be damned if I start running away this late in life," Weiss replies. "After all, I couldn't have come at a better time."

"What do you mean?" Roland asked, noticing that Weiss didn't lock his shackles. "As an older guy, doesn't that make you even more of a target out here?"

"Maybe, maybe not. Times have definitely changed. Many moons ago, I probably would've welcomed any fool to challenge me for what's mine. But things are different, and, naturally, so has my outlook on the world. Hasania has had its fair share of dark days, but the recent attacks are some of the first of their kind," Weiss says as he looks out into the open sea.

"How do you figure? Even with the Empire running things, people still can't get it together out here," Roland thinks out loud. "Good, bad, and everything in between. It seems like people are always going to get into it around here. Surely you've been around long enough to see what I mean firsthand."

"Yes, I have seen a lot, Roland. But this is a far cry from the countless skirmishes that have taken place over the years. The bouts that have taken place in the past had a sense of honor. A sense of dignity. Right or wrong, both sides at least believed they were fighting towards some cause. But unwarranted attacks on the innocent? That takes a special kind of evil."

"I agree. I truly do. I apologize if I upset you," Roland quietly replies. "I guess it's just my nature to question, I suppose."

"Not an issue. I suppose speaking after days alone at sea was just what the doctor ordered," Weiss reassures him. "Regardless of how I feel about this, I pray for good fortune moving forward. Even if I was only able to save you, I'm glad to have made a difference somehow."

"Trust me, Sir. I'm deeply grateful for what you've done and I'll definitely pay it forward," Roland nods. "Wow, that was the best conversation I've had in weeks. Who would have thought?"

"Life's funny like that sometimes, young buck."

"Heh, I'm like twenty-five. That's half your age. How does that make me a young buck?"

"What? How are you like twenty-five? You either are or you aren't. Moreover, twenty-eight would be half my age. How did you make it this far in life?"

"Come on, Craig! We were doing so good until you questioned my math skills. I should have told you how sensitive I am about my—"

"You did no such thing! And Craig? Don't get too comfortable, boy!"

"Boy? I know we're in the south and all, but you really need to be more considerate of how—"

The boat crashed into something. Weiss and Roland saw it had hit a sizable object.

"What do you think it is, Buck?"

"Call me crazy, but it looks like a part of the bridge."

"All the way out here? How is that even possible?"

"I don't know, but I'm going to check it out," Roland says as he leaps from the boat.

Confirming that the surrounding debris was from the Prospear Bridge, Roland calls out to Weiss.

"Bring the boat around right now!"

"What's going on over there, Roland? What did you find?"

"Not a what, old man. More like a who," Roland says as he carries an unconscious individual aboard the ship.

"How this is even possible?" Weiss asks. "That attack was days ago. How could anyone survive floating about for that long?"

"Who knows? I checked his vitals and the kid is barely breathing."

"That's good, it could have been worse. Much worse. Please tend to him while I set a course for home."

"Home? We need to get him to a hospital as soon as possible. If you head back where you found me, then we'll be able to—"

"Be mindful of who's running this ship, Buck. I won't let him die on my watch," Weiss says as he reveals a small crystal. Doing this caused the boat to speed at an incredible rate. Barely able to contain his shock, Roland quickly held on to what he could as they pressed on.

"W-what in the world did you just do, Weiss? You didn't tell me you were some sort of wizard!"

"I'm not. Well, not exactly. Either way, we'll be there shortly. There isn't much I could do for him in the middle of the water, but he'll be in capable hands shortly."

"Hang on, I'm coming too? Whatever happened to having no intentions of bringing me with you?" Roland says, trying to keep his anxiety at bay.

"Clearly there was a change of plans. I don't have time to explain everything right now, but you're only heading there to help with him. That's it, do you understand? No more, no less."

"Of course, of course. Though I have to say given my line of work, I'm dying to do a spread on this. Well, with your blessing, of course."

"Boy, if you so much as say one word about where you're about to go, then I'll see to it that you actually die," Weiss snaps. "Feel free to quote that one!"

"Look, I really thought we were moving forward from the whole 'boy' thing, but if you're really stuck in your ways—"

"Ah, hush! I need to focus on getting us there! Just keep checking on our friend," Weiss orders. "As for your question, I suppose we can discuss more once we…Are you stealing from him?? I knew you were one of those punks!"

"Hey, just calm down! The kid has taken quite a few serious hits, we'll probably be there soon, and I was just checking his tag to see what his blood type is," Roland replies as he provided direct pressure on the wound.

"Hmm, let's see. If worse comes to worst, we have the same type so I could always—"

"Wait, wait. The things that you're doing. You aren't just some journalist, are you? What's going on, Roland?"

"We can talk more once we get there. About everything. But like you said, he's not dying on our watch, Skip."

"Understood, Buck. Was there anything else you were able to find? Anything information that could help once we get there," Weiss asks. "We'll reach the shores as soon."

"Not much, unfortunately. Looking at his wounds, it looks like he went down swinging. They look pretty fresh too. My guess is that they're from the attack on the bridge. Not much, I know, but it looks like this kid put up a hell of a fight. How he's still alive is beyond me."

"Alive for now. Let's not speak so soon. Were you able to get anything else? Anything at all?"

"Oh, right. Just a name from his tag. I know it isn't much, but from what I can make from it…Let's see…Well Skip, it's…K-Keenth. The kid's name is Keenth."

THROUGH THE FOG, PT. I

"Yo, yo! It's Keenth, coming at you live from–Wait that sounds dumb, they could see where I am," the young man thinks to himself. "Well, um, the Training Academy is on holiday break right now, so I decided to check in with you guys out there while I get some well-deserved–"

"Boy," an old man shouts. "If I have to tell you one more time to put that damn camera down and help me with these crates, I swear on everything that–"

"...Well, alright then! It looks like that's all the time we have today, folks. Be easy! Keenth Hedstrom, out!"

It was just another sunny day near the small seaside mountains with Keenth giving Renzel, the village elder, yet another headache.

As he made his way to the back of a cargo airship, Elder Renzel stared at Keenth with a look of confusion and a hint of pity. It was a quiet afternoon in Colonia and it happened to be when shipments would come and go through the quaint island community.

In his time growing up there, Keenth had grown accustomed to the easygoing ways of Colonia and the hard work and determination of the people had influenced him in a very positive way, at least in his opinion.

"Keenth, how many times do I have to tell you not to broadcast every little thing?"

"Oh, come on. It's been months since I've been home and I just wanted to keep the people in the loop," Keenth explains as he loads some boxes, hoping to start a conversation.

"Look, the point is that by the world's standards, we're pretty laid back," Renzel replies. "I just don't want you to get into the habit of thinking the rest of the world is the same."

"Who are you telling? Most of the folks at the Academy act as if they don't have any manners at all. People like you make me want to stay home, you know? This is a nice, easygoing place where you can look at life with a smile—at least I do."

"You have a lot to learn, son. To think that someone like you, from way out here, could qualify for that Academy of theirs. Hey, someone really must be looking out for you up there."

"To be honest, I'm a bit surprised myself. I took the entrance exam to see how I'd do and a few months later, they said that they were interested. The thing is, there is a program for potential attendees outside of the region, and I guess I fit that description, old man."

"Yeah, yeah. Just remember you're a unique individual, Keenth. Just like everyone else."

Keenth laughed. Although many of the people around Colonia

had separate ways of life, the way that they all came together was a lot like family. They were the kind of people who know and understand others which meant a lot to Keenth.

Those were the inhabitants of Colonia. As much as he valued his time back home, Keenth understood that it was his last night before heading back to the Training Academy.

"Hey sorry, but I've gotta rest up. You know, I've got a big day ahead tomorrow."

"I'll check in on you before you head out, yeah?" Elder Renzel looked down, signifying that he got the message.

*

"Units One and Two move in. Unit Three: Stand by until further notice."

"Copy, Sir."

The first group moves around a facility, motioning for the second to follow. They slowly move toward their destination, when, suddenly, the third group makes a call for assistance. The leader of the operation heads back.

"Something isn't right with these chambers; they were still in use. There must be projects dating back to at least five years here," Agent Keyes says as he examines the area.

Senior Agent Lawrence Keyes knows mech-technology like the back of his hand as he is essentially the foundation of what is known around the world as the LanTech Empire.

Agent Keyes has the first two groups standby as he examines the other location with the third. Some of these machines were still warm which signified that they were used in as little as a few hours prior.

This reconnaissance mission dated back about three months and was thought to have been a bust until recently when Agent Keyes had decided to lead the operation.

With a seasoned Agent on the case, it looked promising that they were close to shutting down a major rebel force in northern Tortuga, or so they thought.

"Sir, you should come and look at this!"

"What? This can't be right," Agent Keyes responds, baffled. "Rebels couldn't possibly have the means to…Everyone, get back!"

A terrible explosion sounded around where the first two groups were posted. Was it an ambush? There was sickening smoke that filled the area, a demonic fog looking to blind all around.

"I c-can hardly breathe in here…What's going on? Is this place on fire?" Keenth thinks to himself as he gasps for air.

While he had no clue as to where he is or how he got there, Keenth knew that with each toxic breath he inhales took him closer to the end of his young life. At this point, he is reduced to crawling. With each push, he felt closer to the abyss.

An unknown figure appears then and strikes him. The being was seemingly unfazed by the cloud of death that loomed around them. It must've been some sort of monster: not only for attacking someone that was near death, but for presumably causing this destruction in the first place.

Acting instinctively, Keenth rose to his feet, seeing this as unforgivable. He drew his sword to cut down this nemesis with the last of his ailing strength. As he desperately tries to fight the being, more figures like it appear, signifying the end.

As Keenth closes his eyes expecting the worst, he is left confused as a pale blue flash appears in its presence, suddenly causing the figures to fade, one by one. All that is left is a single hooded figure walking away.

"W-Wait! Don't go—!"

The figure, who apparently was also unaffected by the smoke, turns to Keenth and he catches their eye.

Those eyes—those mysterious eyes—seemed as if they were shining through the fog, but all too quickly, Keenth awakened, bewildered.

It was all a dream. More specifically, a dream that Keenth had been having for several days now.

While the details were generally shrouded by mystery, a feeling of uncertainty lingered.

"No, no, no! I'm gonna be late," Keenth shouts, noticing it is almost time to leave.

Keenth had ended up oversleeping, but since the cargo airship hadn't left yet, he still had a shot making it to Tortuga.

Thinking of Elder Renzel and the others, he said a quiet thank you to himself before boarding.

After looking his boarding pass, he barely made it, but manages to stand in the back, covered with feathers, among other things.

*

In Sadeena, the highly industrialized southern region of Hasania, the atmosphere is far from an easygoing afternoon where one could watch the clouds drift by like empty thoughts.

Here, a young woman pulls into a LanTech Facilitation Building, where she is greeted by a man who just finishes smoking.

"It is pretty weird seeing you early for anything, Giles. Did they tell you there would be a prize if you showed up on time or something?" Agent Connors jokes.

It was always good to use humor in tense situations, especially with this one in particular. Her friend had a subtle distress in his eyes.

"Well, I was in the neighborhood and I figured, why not? That and you can't sit here and tell me this weather isn't as motivational as it gets, right, Jinni?" Agent Giles replies as he looks for another cigarette.

Agent Connors, however, had a slight smirk. The kind where she wanted to show that she was serious, but, at the same time, she knew that some people know just when and how to make others smile.

In her case, Agent Giles was one of those people.

"Hey! We don't have to go through this each and every time: my name is Jennifer. Jennifer! I cannot stand being called that! Besides, someone like me has it hard enough as it is being taken seriously these days," Agent Connors says as she stomps out a discarded cigarette.

"Well, if a nickname is all it takes for people to avoid you, then I guess it's for the best. I mean, look at you! You're a young woman who is in pretty good shape. Not to mention that you have that long dark brown hair that I like so much, a pretty good personality and an even better–"

"Okay, okay I get it," Agent Connors shouts for the sake of stopping him before he got any further. "Say another word and I'll break your jaw! Your call, Ro!"

As other officials were gathering, it seemed like it was time to get to business. They were in an assembly hall within the facility, filled with several LanTech personnel and affiliates.

The meeting was being held by Cordela Lt. Commander, Elite Agent Laurent Masterson.

"As you are all aware, Veteran Agent Lawrence Keyes was murdered not too long ago. Needless to say, this is a massive devastation on all fronts."

"While I didn't know him on a personal level, as some of you may have, with him being such a crucial figure in the LanTech Empire, this is nothing short of a tragedy."

While both Agents Connors and Giles were personally commissioned into the organization years ago, one would think that the Agent Masterson, who was a comrade of Agent Keyes for decades, would project more emotion into his tone. Perhaps that was the true reality of the LanTech Empire.

Draped in their signature black overcoats laced with their silver insignia, an Agent of the LanTech Empire was seen as the personification of authority.

They were well-respected, if not feared, throughout the world.

The truth of the matter was that the LanTech Empire as a whole was a militant force known worldwide, primarily governing in three major regions of Hasania.

Through their crystal-based technology, they were able to pave a new future.

The LanTech Empire was mainly known for its high-tech machinery, primarily used for the preservation of order.

These machines, or simply mechs, were known for their level of destructive power and the onslaught they'd inflict on any who would try to oppose them.

"Old man Keyes, it's a damn shame," Agent Giles says, trying to get Agent Connors to pay attention.

"I know. I still don't believe it, or at least that's what I tell myself. To think a life like his could end in a way like that makes it all seem so pointless."

"Pointless is an understatement. He wasn't just a Senior Agent; he was a dear friend of mine and investigating this attack is a top priority."

The attendees were suddenly being addressed by the voice of Commanding Officer Lansient. Commander Lansient who the embodiment of the LanTech Empire.

Even though he wasn't there in person, the LanTech Commander was a man known for little words, so his inclusion in the meeting alone spoke volumes.

"It wasn't just a loss for me, but for the whole world. Without him, the advancements with mech-based technology would be so minimal that we wouldn't be where we are today. For that, among other things," he continues.

"I am grateful to have known the late Agent Keyes for all of these years," the Commander concludes.

"Understood, Sir. With that, I will address the personnel that will be assigned to the Keyes Investigation," Agent Masterson continues.

"On a similar note, the commemoration ceremony in his name is currently slated to be held at the Hasania Training Academy. We may get some results if we focus on both closely," Agent Masterson says, motioning for the end of the meeting.

Hasania

Cordela Capital City

Tortuga Capital City

Training Academy

Cordela

Cordela Outskirts

Tortuga

Tortuga Outskirts

Prospear Bridge

Port Town

Sadeena Outskirts

Sadeena

Port City

Sadeena Industrial City

Colonia Island

0   100
Miles

THROUGH THE FOG, PT. II

Airships roar through the clear skies and the beauty that is Hasania is within sight. Hasania, the major continent of the east, is filled with luscious forests and magnificent mountains that would set the perfect stage for anyone looking for a new beginning.

Filled with a diverse group of people, the very soul of Hasania is a reflection of its glory. Truly an enchanting sight for any and all who have seen or experienced its regions.

The airships were due to land on the northeast region of Tortuga, far north from Colonia Island. The fact that Keenth was able to reach his destination in a short amount of time was all thanks to the brilliance that is the Airship.

While no one enters the world knowing who they are or what they'll be, it's truly remarkable knowing that minds could change the world in ways that most could ever imagine.

The time has come for Keenth to return to the Hasania Training Academy, the largest centralized training institution within the region that was established to help form the future with the best and brightest Hasanians in the forefront.

Unbeknownst to some, Keenth Hedstrom is quite gifted scoring a 173/200 in his entrance exams with the average score being in the 150s and being a Grade Two swordsman as well, where most recruits barely ranked Grade Three.

"Welcome, all! I hope you all enjoyed your much-deserved time off. We are looking forward to…"

Keenth is seen frantically rushing into the main hall, causing some people to laugh at him, while others look away, embarrassed. Instructor Joseph Adey was none too pleased by the matter, but has come to come to expect this from a young trainee.

It is said that Instructor Adey has been a skilled technician for many years, but has recently opted to spend his tenure in the Training Academy. An older man, Instructor Adey has proven he still has a keen eye on the situation no matter what the circumstance…Or so he thought.

"Well, like I was saying, welcome back. It's been a while, so I'll give you all a quick refresher on things. Sounds good, yeah? Now, if you would please follow me…"

Instructor Adey continues showing the ins and outs of the various halls and chambers that make up the Training Academy. Mechanical models are displayed with honor, as well as photographs of officials, new and old.

As they go on, Keenth takes a few photographs of his own with a disposable camera as if he was a tourist, but his instructor confiscates it from him.

"As you all know, or at least should, the late Agent Keyes of the LanTech Empire was a major benefactor of our Academy. His goal was to educate the future, not help destroy it."

"While we're on the subject, there will be a ceremony held here in honor of him in a few days. It will be a major event, so please prepare accordingly."

"Sorry, Sir, but who did you say that the ceremony for," Keenth blurts, proving his obliviousness to everything that was clearly explained to the group just moments earlier.

Instructor Adey sighs in disappointment, but before he can respond, an irritated young man who was sitting on top of a high banister went out of his way to finally speak his mind about the Keenth's absent-mindedness.

"Wow, he literally just said it was for Agent Keyes, I mean are you even listening? Because there is no way—"

"And here we go. Is there a problem there, pal?"

"For someone to just—wait, do you have something smart to say? As I've said before and I'll probably say another thousand times, I am much more qualified to be here than you are. Something that you couldn't possibly comprehend and—"

This was nothing new to Instructor Adey. Despite being classmates, the two were known to argue over every little thing. This was much to the amusement of the other attendees as well the instructor until Adey himself eventually decided to step in.

"Paul! Island boy! Er, I mean Keenth! That's enough!"

The others collectively laugh as Keenth and Paul stare one another down. Paul Fehren, arguably being the more mature one, decides to take the high road and walks on ahead muttering to himself.

"Whatever…"

Keenth, deciding to take the low road, wanted to have the last word which was muttered ever so quietly under his breath.

"Yeah, you keep walking, bitch..."

Their fight continues on until an older woman lightly slaps both Keenth and Paul on the back of their heads. Keenth was quick to question who would dare do such a thing to him of all people, but Paul pulled him aside.

"Quit it, you idiot! That is Madam Chambers, so show some respect!"

"The madam, what now?"

"Seriously, how many times do we have to explain this?" Paul said as he raises his head up. "She is the High Council of Tortuga. She is more or less the leader of this entire region!"

"Actually," Madam Chambers said as her two subordinates followed her.

"While I appreciate the introduction, young man, just know that it takes a village. Like when it came to this Academy for example. It was mainly established thanks in huge part to the support of the late Agent Keyes. He was a man who greatly contributed in making this happen."

Madam Chambers turns round and surprisingly hits Instructor Adey as well.

"What are you teaching these kids anyhow, Mr. Adey?"

"To be fair, this is their first day back from break."

"Well, I wanted to take a look at the grounds for a bit seeing how I unfortunately won't be able to make it to the ceremony."

"Really? That's rather unexpected. He was a close friend of yours, wasn't he?"

She looked down for a moment and didn't answer. Madam Rebecca Chambers was definitely up there, age-wise that is, arguably older than

Instructor Adey. It seemed the older you are, the more accustomed you are to life's uncertainties. "Well, that'll be in a few days and I will be sending others else in my stead," Madam Chambers says, trying to get the attention of the two who accompanied her.

"With that, I'll be off. Until we meet again, good luck to all of you! I'm sure you will continue making us proud."

Madam Chambers was accompanied by two individuals. One was a young woman with long dark hair with sharp hazel eyes who seemed none too thrilled about being there.

The other woman was around the same age, but a little taller with dark blonde hair and soft blue eyes who looked as if she had just woken up moments earlier.

They were two fairly distinctive personalities clearly, with the only common link being that they were both Executive Assistants to Madam Chambers.

As opposed to LanTech's militant facade, these two opted to wear a relaxed navy-blue uniform, a garb significantly more inviting compared to LanTech's, which may be a reflection on how they were viewed throughout Tortuga, if not Hasania altogether.

"As for you two, I'd like some field work done. While I'm sure LanTech is leading its own investigation, only so much will be released to the public and that's where you come in. Pay close attention to this as I'm sure there is more than meets the eye."

Instructor Adey has the trainees go on ahead and Madam Chambers asks her associates for a moment so that she could have a few words in private.

"I figured you would do as much," Instructor Adey said. "I guess I'm wiser than you assume. That aside, do you have a minute?"

"Of course, what is on your mind?"

"You know as well as I do that an event like this raises huge awareness and other officials may be at risk–those in LanTech, the Academy, and warriors alike."

"I know, but are you suggesting that rebels are really at risk as well? For all we know, they were the ones behind Keyes' attack. Also, I think working alongside the Empire would be best for what's going on right now."

"I wouldn't be so sure. After all, I wanted our own investigation without LanTech for a reason. That and a rebel attack? I mean sure, that's expected but..."

"Wait, you couldn't mean..."

"Well, we still need to analyze all of the possibilities, no matter how unbelievable or trivial. Either way, I would like for you to do me a favor during the ceremony as well."

THROUGH THE FOG, PT. III

The sun shines on an underdeveloped island off of the northern coast of Tortuga where the location of the Keyes Attack is being investigated.

An individual Airship lands nearby and as the Agent demounts, his subordinates stop to give a briefing on what they have uncovered so far.

"Thank you for coming, Sir! We've found some—"

"I got it, I got it. The information that you all would see as exclusive is pretty much common knowledge by the time it reaches me. Let's see: You still have no serials, no prints, and all available censors were disabled roughly two hours before the incident, correct?"

"Y-Yes, Sir..."

The Agent, noticing that the others felt a bit discouraged by how quickly he was able to discern what they had spent hours putting together in just a few moments, decided to change his tone a little bit for the better.

"But, this is good work considering. At least a case like this keeps us out of the office, so that's a plus, right?"

The small talk didn't seem to be working.

"Oh, come on," Agent Fallon says, "Does everyone always have to be so gloomy when they are around me? Please don't say it has anything to do with my glasses?"

The rest of the group eventually lightened up. Agent David Fallon, much like Agents Connors and Giles, was also mentored by Agent Keyes.

Initially looking to work under one of the three regional High Councils, he opted to join the LanTech Empire after a personal recommendation from Agent Keyes.

"Y-You knew him, right?" a nervous aide asks as she hands him a report.

"Agent Keyes? Yes, he was the kind of person who would make you feel like he was one of your own. Like family, you know. Figuratively speaking, obviously."

"Hey, speaking of family, don't you have a brother or something?" another aide blurts out, causing the others to get quiet. "Hey... Is it something I said?"

Agent Fallon's usual expression of callousness returned all too soon signifying that the time for small talk was over and they had a job, no, a duty to fulfill.

*

As Agent Fallon looks up to the clouds thinking silently to himself, the focus is on one of the study areas of the Training Academy where Keenth is seen doing the same.

It has been a couple of days since he returned and since then, Keenth has been hard at work getting back to the basics.

"I think I finally decided on a specialty," Keenth tells an uninterested Paul. "It took a couple weeks of time off back home to figure it out, but I think I'm going to give logistics a go. How about you, are you in?"

"I wouldn't recommend a specialty that you can't spell without looking it up," Paul smugly responds. "Besides you know there's more to logistics than kicking boxes around, don't you?"

"Hah! Coming from the clown who thinks that they have a shot at being an Agent one day? You have a lot of nerve!"

"I'll have you know that training certifications from the Academy will help me reach my goals sooner than you think. Don't be surprised if you're taken down by me one day, jackass!"

"On what grounds?"

"Well, I don't know, probably for being content with being called a jackass?"

"Really, now? Well, I guess you're gonna find out the only thing worse than being a jackass is getting your ass beat by one because—"

To absolutely no one's surprise, Keenth and Paul got into yet another scuffle. This time, however, it was decided that changes needed to be made to ensure that both trainees would fully reach their potential.

But as fate would have it, they were not thrilled with the changes and Keenth was exceptionally vocal about it.

"Paul?? Why in the hell do I have to room with him?" Keenth protests in front of Instructor Adey who clearly didn't care either way.

"You know this is the kind of stuff that starts wars, right? You couldn't have possibly made a bigger mistake," Paul adds.

"As much as I hate the simpleton, he's right. Sir, with all due respect, if this is supposed to be some sort of lesson then, trust me, I've learned it. But I can't bear the thought of being that close to someone, no, something like that for months! This is completely unethical!"

"Hey, you know what, I have to agree with you for once there, man," Keenth agrees. "I guess it's gotta be a pretty crazy situation where we would...Wait-wait-wait! What in the hell do you mean by thing! You...You're the reason why I drink!"

"Underage drinking is something we at the Training Academy take very seriously," Instructor Adey quips.

"Ah, just kidding, Sir. H-Ha...joke...yeah," Keenth quietly states.

Instructor Adey stood up leaving the two students anxious as to what his final word on the situation would be. His say would very much determine their fate as trainees moving forward.

"Here it is. While I wish I could take credit for pairing the two of you together, it is a bit more complicated than that. While Keenth here was seen as fully capable during the entrance exams, his progress in the Academy hasn't exactly reflected that."

"That being said, Paul didn't necessarily score as well in the entrance exams, but he is definitely in the top of the class, so it's fairly balanced," Instructor Adey continues to explain.

"We are looking for trainees to be on the same level, so hopefully the two of you rub off on each other the right way. That or at the very least manage to get you two to drop out on your own terms, whichever works best for you."

Seeing what was before them, Keenth and Paul begrudgingly agree to put their minor differences aside and look back on it all only to laugh it off.

"See? Everything works out," Instructor Adey says as he motions for someone to enter the room. "Oh, which reminds me: As a training facility, we will do everything in our power to help you succeed. I made a few calls and was fortunate enough to have—"

"Aamina's the name! Leading's the game! Assistant Student Affairs Liaison, nice to meet you," a lively young woman boldly announces to Keenth and Paul.

"Wait, no, on second thought Ms. Aamina works best since I am your senior, but not senior-senior because I'm only a few years older than you...Well, a couple years...Anyway, I'm looking forward to keeping you two on track!"

"Assistant *to the* Student Affairs Liaison," Instructor Adey sighs.

"Well, it looks like someone isn't a stranger to coffee," Paul says jokingly.

"Yeah, I'm pretty sure that this lady has more than a few screws loose," Keenth says with a smirk on his face.

"I'll smack the life out of them, Adey! I'll seriously do it and you know it! I'm not afraid to go back to probation either," Aamina states as the instructor tries to calm her down.

In a brief, yet humbling experience, the two trainees were speechless.

"Perfect! Now you two come close so that I can take a photo for our newsletter. First impressions are everything," Aamina exclaims.

"N-now hold on just a minute...We didn't sign up for this!"

While things began to get better between Keenth and Paul, it was just a matter of time before the two friendly rivals would eventually reemerge to their much more fitting roles as bitter enemies yet again.

The next morning, they were up bright and early to warm up for the day ahead.

"Whoa, that tree's huge! Hey Paul, I've been meaning to ask you. Why is it that you're always on top of high places like that?"

"Funny you say that, because I'm pretty sure I've been meaning to tell you. How about you just hold your breath until I do, okay?"

"Your mother never hugged you, am I right?"

"You see, I think better when I'm above ground." Paul laughed.

"It helps me get my mind off of things, and it takes quite a bit of concentration to stay here, so if you understand—"

"Yeah," Keenth replies while sitting on top of a much higher branch much to Paul's surprise. Before he could ask, Keenth goes on, "You see, I'm not too sure how it is around here, but something as simple as tree climbing to clear your head shouldn't be treated as a science, you know."

"I guess you're right. Listen, I've been meaning to ask you this, but why exactly did you come to the Academy? No offense, but you don't really seem like the military type, and it's not like you could go and tell me that you're more inclined to the medical field because you and I both know that would be a lost cause by now."

Keenth thought about it and jumped down the tree with relative ease.

"Funny you say that because I'm pretty sure I've been meaning to tell you too. Just do me a favor and play in traffic for a few hours in the meantime, alright?"

Paul laughed again. Most people have come to see Keenth as a bit of a clown, but, unlike them, Paul has come to see that he definitely has a lot more to him.

"Actually, I'm the kind of person who doesn't really depend on a description to see how a person is and what they're really about."

"We haven't known each other for too long, but give it some time and, from there, you could figure who I am a lot better than me trying to explain it to you."

Paul figured out how he lives by a similar philosophy as well. Life has a funny way of teaching people a thing or two.

*

Agent Connors found herself designated as the Lead Agent of the Keyes Investigation. It made sense seeing how she was the Senior Intel Agent of the LanTech Empire.

Naturally, she requested that Agent Giles, who she sees not only as her most trustworthy ally, but an invaluable friend, be onboard the investigation.

Unfortunately for her, the word trustworthy didn't bear the same significance as it did with Agent Giles, seeing how words like tardy and dismissive would best describe him and his actions outside of fieldwork.

"You know if you're going to suggest where we go during this investigation, the least you could do is show up," Agent Connors thinks to herself.

Agent Connors wasn't as familiar with Tortuga as Agent Giles and found herself damning his free-spiritedness which could, in fact, from be a bit of envy on her part.

Although he is a part of an organization as prestigious as LanTech Empire, Agent Giles was always one to follow his gut in everything he'd do, as opposed to doing things by the book.

This understandably led to him being well-received among his peers more than the senior officials of the Empire, that was, aside from Agent Keyes.

Agent Keyes was definitely what many would see as a mentor to both Agents Connors and Giles. Understandably, this investigation is more personal than professional for the pair.

"If I remember correctly, I'm not too far away from my destination.

So, if anything, I could meet up with him and the others shortly."

What Agent Connors didn't see coming was an anonymous call that addressed her by her full name? Startled, she landed her airship and went back to the Agent state-of-mind.

"Who is this?"

"Don't look now, but you're being followed."

Before she could continue, she was surprised by a sudden tap on her window and found herself gasping. This made it all too apparent that even an Agent such as herself could lose their cool in certain situations.

The mystery behind the voice turned out to be a colleague who had an innocent smirk on his face, despite startling his comrade.

"Damn, David! You scared me to death, you moron!"

"My apologies, Agent Connors. I don't know what the big deal is. I thought it was my obligation to show concern to a fellow Agent. How come anytime one tries to build bridges, others divide? When one wishes for peace, others collide? How come—"

"You don't just keep your mouth shut," Agent Connors says as she begrudgingly accepts his apology.

Interestingly enough, Agent David Fallon was another individual who Agent Keyes had inspired through his tenure within the LanTech Empire.

As such, had a close connection with Agent Connors, although it wasn't as close as the one she shared with Agent Giles.

Despite that, Agent Connors has come to respect Agent Fallon's work ethic which is a complete contrast to that of Agent Giles'.

Agent Fallon is known for standing up for what he believes in which oftentimes coincides with the actions and beliefs of the LanTech Empire.

Among the group of known officials, he would be considered most suitable for the highly esteemed position of an Elite Class Agent which is a position held by no more than a handful of individuals, Commanding Officer Lansient included.

While Agent David Fallon himself is seen as what one would want to achieve if they were part of the Empire, his younger brother, Agent James Fallon, is anything but that.

Despite sharing a similar appearance with dark eyes and a rather distinguished facade, the two couldn't be any different, as seen by their attitudes and their reputations.

While the elder Fallon is seen as a well-kept, conventional-minded individual, James has earned the reputation of being a rather flashy, free-spirited person, especially compared to LanTech standards.

But it could very well just be about comparing scholarly and cocky mindsets respectively. Keeping in character, Agent Fallon was quick to get straight to the situation at hand.

"It is good to hear that you are leading the investigation, Agent Connors. To be honest, I was concerned that if the wrong people were involved, then we wouldn't get anywhere with this. Or worse, that it would all be for nothing."

"Those are my thoughts exactly. We don't have too much to work with so if anything, we need the most suitable people on the job. Speaking of which, do you have any idea where Agent Giles is? He's supposed to meet me here."

"Oh, that reminds me, he asked me to pass this to you:

Jinni, I'll be doing some work around Tortuga, so don't wait up on me.-R. Giles

"That idiot," Agent Connors thinks to herself.

"Ah, that is a lot like him, after all. You know, I wish I could be of some help with you two out here, but I am still working on the forensic side of the Keyes Incident."

"While this case means a lot to me, I wouldn't want my personal feelings to tamper with the investigation in any way."

"I understand what you mean. Besides, I heard that your brother is being put on board for the investigation. It's anyone's guess if he's even suitable for his current job," Agent Connors replies, trying to get a few words out of Agent Fallon about his brother and her potentially new subordinate.

Agent Fallon tried his best to front with a half-hearted smile, but even then, he couldn't help but laugh at the fact that James was a part of the investigation, let alone affiliated with the LanTech Empire whatsoever.

"I need you to do me a favor and look after him for me when you can. Besides the fact he's a Junior Official without too much experience, he still bears the Fallon name."

This was strange to Agent Connors seeing how Agent Fallon was willing to openly express concern over his younger brother.

Even though he'd try his hardest not to show it, Agent Fallon still had a place for his sibling in his mind, despite their differences.

"No problem and thanks for the heads up, David."

"Oh…Yeah, about that. It's Agent Fallon. Remember: Agent Fallon."

"Right, right. Take care, Agent Fallon," Agent Connors replies.

All too quickly, Agent Connors was reminded about the state of mind while in the LanTech Empire.

At times she would question joining in the first place, but she would come to understand her reasons as time went on.

THROUGH THE FOG, PT. IV

T he morning of the commemoration ceremony finally approaches. Keenth and the others prepare for what was looking to be a very eventful gathering.

Given the amount of influence Agent Keyes had on the world, many paths are expected to cross on this fateful day.

"I hate wearing ties," Keenth says as he adjusts his collar.

"I wouldn't be surprised if this was the first time you were wearing one."

"And how could you tell? Better yet, who asked you in the first place, Paul?"

"Well, maybe it's the fact that your tie is on backwards for starters?"

"You know, we are going to fight for real one day, and I'd be a liar if I was to tell you that I'm not looking forward to it."

"Gents! How are we looking?" Aamina asks, wearing a formal

black gown. "Well, what do you think?"

"Meh," Keenth and Paul reply simultaneously.

"Well, I think you look like a very dignified young woman."

"And you are?"

"Ah, of course. I'm Connors. Agent Jennifer Connors. Pleased to meet you all."

"It was rude of me. After all, I should've addressed you as an Agent based on your LanTech lapel pin," Paul replies.

"Please, please…Today you can just call me Jennifer."

"Ah, Jennifer as in Jinni? That's a lot easier to remember. By the way, I'm Keenth…Nice to meet ya!"

"W-What did you just call me?

"I-I'm sorry," Aamina said, trying to give Keenth a hint. "Our friend here is a little…yeah…"

"No, it's not a big deal. It's just that, well, I detest that nickname to no end, ha ha," Agent Connors says as she tries to keep her anger at bay.

"If you don't mind me asking, what brings you up here this morning?" Paul says.

"Nothing in particular. It's just that I haven't really looked around at the Training Academy in a while. It is pretty interesting seeing new faces in a familiar setting. In fact, Lawrence took me and a few others on many tours of this facility many moons ago."

"I'm sorry, but Lawrence?"

"Oh, sorry, I was referring to the late Agent Keyes."

"Wow, you must have known him pretty well," Keenth interjects.

"I sure did. If it wasn't for him, I probably wouldn't have joined the LanTech Empire in the first place."

"We are really sorry for your loss," Aamina adds.

"That's very kind of you, thank you. You know, seeing the Academy as it is today shaping the lives of young people like you brings me hope. A reminder that, even though Agent Keyes may not be with us in the literal sense, he still lives on through people like you."

"Really, now? Do you think so," Paul asks.

"Of course!"

"What about me?" Keenth butts in.

"I-I think I'm going to head downstairs now. Nice meeting you. See you all at the ceremony."

The ceremony begins and the guests are very well-dressed for the special occasion. Among them, three LanTech Agents make an appearance, among some of the highest ranked.

While many in the outside world do not know all of their true identities and strengths, they are still respected and revered individuals.

Opening remarks are provided by Agent Connors. Aside from the Commanding Officer, she is one of the most well-recognized Agents of recent times.

That combined with the fact she knew Agent Keyes personally made her leading the ceremony an obvious choice.

"Hello, good morning, and thank you all for attending. We shall begin the ceremony but first, allow me to introduce you to my colleagues: Agents Elise Van, James Fallon, and of course myself, Jennifer Connors."

"Agent Giles was scheduled to appear and deeply regrets that he was unable to, so he sends his thoughts and condolences."

Agent Connors and the others speak about the life and times of Agent Lawrence Keyes while the guests listen respectfully.

"Some of you missed the privilege of meeting an astounding individual on all fronts," Agent Van adds on.

"The ones responsible for this heinous crime have no doubt robbed a generation. But let's carry on in his footsteps so that through our own actions, he lives on."

Pride. Honor. Resolve. All of these factors are important for any member of society and generally speaking for a true individual such as Agent Keyes. He was those words personified.

With that, the ceremony quietly ended. Groups of people meet with the Agents and other officials commenting on the ceremony and Agent Keyes in general.

Keenth and the others are in the lower lobby conversing in idle chitchat. He reflects on the words about Agent Keyes as Aamina approaches.

"Is everything alright, Keenth?"

"Me? Yeah, I'm fine, Ms. Aamina. It's just that, I don't know. After hearing about the kind of legacy people leave behind here, I wonder if maybe coming out here was a waste of time."

"Don't say that, Keenth. You've got us. You, me, Paul…We're here for each other, remember?"

"Yeah, it's just…I don't know…"

"You sound pretty stressed, man. Maybe you outta spar a bit. You know, unwind."

Keenth and Aamina stand puzzled as the mysterious individual continues on.

"What's with the look? You're Keenth as in Keenth Hedstrom, right? Your sword was in the armory so I figured you know…Check it out to pass the time. A bit weird, but you don't have an issue with that, do you?"

"That sword, my sword, was a gift. Putting your hands on what isn't yours is not just weird, it's asking for trouble, don't you think?"

Keenth says with anger in his voice.

"Fair point, but as I'm one of the youngest LanTech Agents in the Empire's history, pleased to meet you by the way, don't see it as a bad thing," Agent James Fallon responds.

"After all, for me to reach out to a trainee like yourself means that you may have the potential to join the ranks of the Invincible Empire one day."

"Which is something that would be more suitable to discuss down the line with the Assistant Student Affairs Liaison," Aamina intervenes.

"Assistant to the Student Affairs Liaison. But look, kid, I didn't mean to tick you off or anything. I'll put this back in the armory and we'll pretend this conversation never happened."

"No, I'm good. Besides, pretending something didn't happen is almost as bad as flaunting your credentials to a teenager," Keenth replies.

"What was that, kid?"

"I said what I said, Sir–"

"Well, goddamn! Alright, wow, alright, I haven't introduced myself: I'm Fallon. Agent James Fallon. Now we go tit for tat all day or we could make this a mentorship session, seeing how we're all in high spirits all of a sudden," Agent Fallon shouts, failing to keep himself calm.

"Yeah, some mentorship sounds really good right about now," Keenth says as he quickly snatches his sword from Agent Fallon. "I would love to kill time…among other things."

"Sure, buddy, that's your call," Agent Fallon says as he prepares himself. "I feel as though I should warn you that as far as lessons go, you shouldn't expect me to go easy."

"Don't worry, I can handle myself."

"Great to hear," Agent Fallon replied with a smirk. "Great to hear…"

Keenth and Agent James Fallon stare each other down with their swords drawn in the courtyard of the Academy. Both of them are intensely probing for the right moment to strike.

"Hey, kid, what's the deal with you staring into the clouds like that?"

Before Keenth could react, Agent Fallon was behind Keenth, beginning his attack. Instinctively, Keenth was able to block the strike and regain his composure.

"This guy is fast," Keenth thinks to himself as he tries to find an opening. "If anything, he is underestimating me, so I should use that to my advantage. Okay, here I go!"

Keenth rushed with a swing to the right, clearly missing his intended target.

"Whoa, that was a pretty heavy swing there, kid. I thought we were just messing around here?"

"I could say the same to you, Agent!"

Keenth repeated the attack, only this time, he swung to the left giving Agent Fallon but a split second to react.

"I have to hand it to you, swinging the way you did earlier so that I would think you were a lefty. Not bad. Not bad at all," Agent Fallon says.

"If I could speak my mind here, I'll tell you that you made that obvious when you actually swung, runt. You couldn't be that great of a swordsman with that kind of style."

"Wait, how did you…?"

"Does it even matter? Relax, relax…I'm part of the Empire. I'm one of the good guys, remember?"

Deciding to step things up, Agent Fallon rushed in violently, shoving Keenth forward. Before Keenth could plan his counter, his opponent was beside him and repeated this.

Keenth was pushed several feet away, causing him to crash to the ground. At this point, it was clear that Agent Fallon was using excessive force, as seen with the wound on Keenth's forehead.

Agent Fallon continued the rapid blows until it was clear that Keenth was becoming disoriented.

"You are painfully slow, kid! If this is the best the Academy has to offer then—"

In a fit of rage, Keenth angrily swung his sword with both arms and, with a torrent of energy sped towards Agent Fallon. Unable to completely dodge the attack, Agent Fallon thwarted it with his right arm.

The sound of the impact was powerful enough to cause several windows in the surrounding area to shatter while the spectators looked on in amazement as the shards rained down in the courtyard.

"Wow...That was some attack. It looks like I was right...you definitely are a special one, alright," Agent Fallon says to himself as he examined his wounded wrist.

Realizing that he was injured by Keenth in front of the others was a massive blow to his ego and Agent Fallon could hardly contain his usual careless front.

The attack, however, drained Keenth, who almost dropped his sword. He was just as surprised about what had happened and Agent Fallon made his way towards him.

"Now that the gloves are off, let's make things interesting..."

Agent Fallon rushes towards Keenth with an attack aimed at the young trainee's neck.

The onlookers are astonished at seeing Agent Connors blocking

Agent Fallon's attack barehanded as Aamina rushes to help Keenth.

"Keenth! Are you alright?"

"M-Ms. Aamina? Yeah, I'm fine. Or at least I think I am…"

"Don't worry about it. Do you have any idea of what you did back there?"

"I-I don't' know…It just happened, I—"

"What the hell were you thinking?" Agent Connors says as she lowers Agent Fallon's blade.

"Oh, come on! He attacked me first! See? I'm bleeding and everything!"

"Agent Fallon, you are part of the LanTech Empire and it would be in your best interest to carry yourself in a respectful manner. Do you understand me?"

"Give me a break! You know, I can't say I remember too much about my mom, but I don't think I'd be wrong in thinking that her nagging sounded a lot like yours."

"I asked if you understood, Agent Fallon??"

"Yes, Agent Connors."

"Keenth, how are you?" Agent Connors asks, examining his wound. "You gave us quite a scare there. We'd better get you some medical attention. That cut of yours looks pretty bad."

"I can help," Aamina volunteers. "I can fix an injury like that no problem!"

The group moved to the upper level of the Academy where Aamina is seen tending to Keenth's wounds, while Agent Connors speaks to Agent Fallon in another room.

At this point in the day, luckily most of the guests had left the Academy, seeing how the ceremony was over.

"You used quite a bit of force, Agent Fallon."

"Yeah, but you know I was holding back earlier, of course. I was just having a little fun, is all."

"Agent Fallon about before, there's no need for me to publicly berate you. At the same time if you openly object to a senior Agent's orders then…"

"No, I hear you loud and clear. I was the one acting out of line. Sorry for that. Agent Connors, just between us, what did you think of what happened earlier?"

"I'm not too sure I understand what you're asking. If anything, it was reckless and there are a few broken windows to prove that."

"Who cares about the windows," Agent Fallon exclaims. "They can be replaced. I'm talking about the fight; do you think they were more impressed with me or the kid?"

"I'm going to act as if I'm not getting the vibe of you treating what happened earlier as a popularity contest, Agent Fallon."

"Sorry to interrupt, but it looks like my guy gave you quite an injury. If it means anything to you, I scolded him already, but between us, you really had it coming," Aamina bluntly states. Agent Connors laughs, while an embarrassed Agent Fallon tries to keep a straight face.

*

That night at the Tortuga Forensics Facility, Agent David Fallon is reviewing a stack of documents. A group of assistants request permission to enter, claiming to have found something very crucial to the investigation.

What they have appears to have been surveillance data. Agent Fallon and the others watch the footage. At first it appears to be nothing, but the audio feed of the scene is of the attack on Agent Keyes' group.

Not too long afterwards, a long silence follows and a seemingly random sequence of numbers appear on the screen.

Suddenly, an image of a metallic mask cryptically flashes before the screen and then numbers return. Then, the tape stops.

"Take this to Agent Connors' team for analysis immediately," Agent Fallon orders.

As the aides began to follow through with the order, Agent Fallon requested to see the video again. He studied it a few more times before he came to his conclusion.

"Those weren't random numbers. Those are sets of times and dates…And coordinates. There's going to be another attack."

"What? You can't be serious, Sir! Where??"

"Clear the Academy."

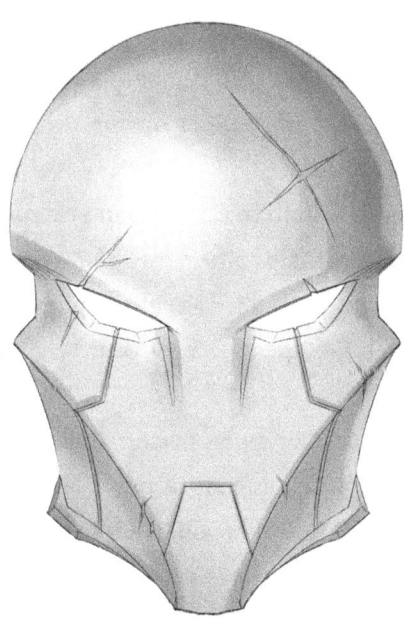

THROUGH THE FOG, PT. V

Night falls where a full moon shines on the Training Academy. Keenth reflects on the events that took place earlier in the day.

"So, when you can't climb trees, you stand on rooftops," Paul asks as he accompanies Keenth upstairs

"Yeah, I guess you're right," Keenth replies. "Paul, you were watching before with the Agent, weren't you? What happened? What did I do?"

"Man, you're asking the wrong person. That was like something out of a movie. Your guess is as good as mine. Not pissed or anything, but it would be nice to know that you had it in you, Keenth. Why did you keep that to yourself?"

"Huh? I don't know what you are talking about. The last thing I wanted to do here at this Academy is cause any trouble."

"Trouble? Dude sparring or not, you were able to strike a LanTech Agent. Do you think something like that happens every day?"

"I wonder what's going to happen next?" Keenth thinks out loud. "Paul, do you think the ones running this place will kick me out or something. That's the last thing that I want."

"You'll cross that bridge when you get there, Keenth. But if it comes down to it, you know that I'll be there to vouch for you. That and at the very least, you should probably reconsider your specialty here because—"

A massive explosion violently trembles the Academy. Before Keenth or Paul could fully process what was going on, two more explosions go off and screams are heard throughout the area.

Paul glances at Keenth and quickly tells him focus on himself and to get to safety while avoiding the main halls. Keenth hesitates, but Paul doesn't waver.

"You're out of your mind if you think I'll run off without making sure that the others are okay, Paul!"

Paul reluctantly agrees and the two begin searching until Keenth looks back only to find Paul surrounded by what could only be described as living shadows.

"Paul, look out!"

As Paul hears Keenth's warning, an explosion went off where he stood. At that moment, Keenth heard a loud, but familiar cry for help.

"Keenth, Paul…Leave…Leave while you can…"

"Ms. Aamina…? Aamina, where are you? AAMINA!"

As other explosions went off, Keenth's fears were realized when he could no longer hear her voice.

"I c-can hardly breathe in here…What's going on? Is this place on fire," Keenth thinks to himself as he gasps for air.

While he had no clue as to what was going on exactly, he knew with each toxic breath he inhaled, he was closer to death. At this point, he was reduced to crawling and, with each push, he felt closer to the abyss.

"No, no, no…I've seen this before!! I've gotta wake up, I just gotta wake up!"

As it has played out in his dreams before, a mysterious shadow appears only to strike the young man while he's down.

This being was seemingly unfazed by the cloud of death that loomed above them. It must've been some sort of monster.

Not only for attacking someone that was near death, but for presumably causing the fatal events to occur in the first place.

Acting instinctively, Keenth rises to his feet seeing this being as unforgivable. He draws his sword to cut down this nemesis with the last of his ailing strength.

As he desperately tries to fight the being, more figures like it appear, signifying the end of the young man.

"No…This can't be happening! Somebody, anybody, please help us—"

As Keenth pleads for his life, he sees a single hooded figure standing in the distance. Amidst the chaos, a savior enters.

"You…Who are—?"

There is no response. The hooded figure moves towards Keenth and helps him off the ground. As the assailants take note of this, they rush towards the two, but are stopped once the floor beneath the enemies collapses.

More assailants try to attack from behind, but they too are stopped when a wall suddenly comes up from the ground. The wall, however, appears to be a stone-like substance which greatly confused Keenth.

"W-who are you? How did you do that?"

Before Keenth could question the mysterious one any further, the assailants broke through the wall with more numbers on their side. It looked grim for the newly formed pair until the mysterious one finally spoke.

"Your questions will have to wait until later. Just stay by me for now."

The ally then put their hand on Keenth's shoulder and concentrated their aura on their two fingers. Without a moment to waste, the ally placed their fingers on their forehead just as another massive explosion went off on that floor.

*

Agents Jennifer Connors and James Fallon race back towards the Academy on her airship. Though it was late at night, the flames engulfing their destination were unmistakable

"You can't be serious. An attack on the Academy of all places?"

"But why today of all days? Do you think it has anything to do with the ceremony earlier? That and how exactly did you receive this information in the first place, Agent Fallon?"

"Like I said, this information was forwarded from my brother's research team!"

"Right, right. Information that was oddly sent directly to you and not me for some reason…"

"Seriously? I don't think now's the time, Agent Connors—"

Agent Fallon was cut off at the sight of an explosion that destroyed nearly half of the Academy right before their eyes.

The aftershock was so intense that their airship had to redirect the course to avoid putting themselves in danger.

Agent Connors looks on in shock as Agent Fallon notices that the smoke coming from the site gave the same image of the ominous mask seen in the surveillance video.

*

As day breaks, Keenth recovers. Unsure of where he was or what had happened, he sees the hooded figure looking off into where the Training Academy once stood intact.

Despite what had happened, Keenth was somewhat skeptical of his mysterious savior.

"Who are you? What is going on here?" Keenth presses on, only to receive no response.

"Hey, I asked you a question!" Keenth asks as he grabs their shoulder. As he moves back, he accidentally pulls down the hood and, to his surprise, reveals a young girl with short brown hair.

Confused, Keenth continued to stare into her eyes, but is stopped short when she finally speaks.

"What's with the look? You know for someone who was just saved, I would think you'd be just a bit more grateful, Keenth. After all, you're not the only one with dreams," she replies with a smile.

"The name's Cory by the way, Cory Daken...Pleasure to save you!"

*

"This is W-NJFM here with our top story: Reports of an attack on the Hasania Training Academy just a few hours ago has local authorities baffled as to what the motive may have been and what was used in such a large-scale attack. While information is limited at this time, the death toll is believed to be in the hundreds. We'll have more on this story after the break."

"That's horrible," Aya says as she studies the images of the attack. "This story is all over the news. It's getting much more coverage than the Keyes Investigation."

"That's understandable. Naturally, LanTech would want to keep a story about a Veteran Agent and his team being attacked under wraps, but an attack on the Training Academy? What is the world coming to," Madam Chambers replies from behind her desk.

Madam Chambers called for a meeting with Aya and Beth to discuss their progress with the Keyes Investigation. Due to the unfortunate turn of events, Madam Chambers and the others knew that they had to change strategy.

"So, what do you expect us to do now, Ma'am?" Aya asks.

"We follow from a distance. Take what you can from the media, but don't be too reliant on their reports, if you understand what I'm saying. Remember that it hasn't been too long since we were at the Academy that has been attacked, so be careful out there."

"While your words are appreciated Madam Chambers, that didn't exactly answer our question. That includes you as well, after all," Beth adds.

"Ah, you got me. If you really need to know, I'm going to reach out to a couple of people who can help with both the investigation and the recent attack," Madam Chambers replies as she puts on her overcoat.

"Interesting. I guess we didn't know you were that well-connected, respectfully speaking, of course," Aya says, stepping up to leave.

"Just because I'm a little older, it doesn't mean I don't have my sources," Madam Chambers responds with a smile.

*

"So, your name's Cory, right?"

"Yup."

"And you saved me from the Academy?"

"Mhm."

"And I'm supposed to follow you because you were told to through a dream?"

"Hmm, something like that, yeah."

"You really expect me to believe all of that? You come here covering yourself in a hood and dressed in a dark-blue robe like you are dressing up as some kind of mage or something…What are you, like twelve? Go back home, I've gotta find the guy who actually saved me."

"First of all, I'm fourteen, not twelve. Second, do you seriously doubt that I saved you? You've never seen me around the Academy, so how is it so hard to believe that I was sent here to help you. You know this attitude of yours is really starting to get under my skin, so let's just head out of here."

"Do you hear yourself right now? I'm not going anywhere with you!"

"Ah, right. The Training Academy that you are a part of has been attacked and you somehow ended up miles from there completely unscathed. You're just going to be a miraculous survivor who's just gonna sit around pretending like everything is alright, right? That's a great story, Keenth."

"No…Just be quiet. And don't call me a survivor because the other ones are alive, I just know it."

"Really? Is that what you're telling yourself? Sorry to say it, but everyone you came across in there is gone. I didn't risk my life for a person who is going to sit around pretending like that isn't true."

"If that's the case, then why didn't you help them? If you knew this was going to happen, then why me? Why did you just save me?"

"Sorry, I don't have an answer for that."

"And why not?" Keenth snaps.

"Because I'm not the one who had the dream, okay? I was sent here by a man named Lord Haden."

"Haden? Who is that?"

"Lord Haden, the Sage of Hatre."

"Wait, Sage? Hatre? What are you talking about?"

"Listen, we don't have time to talk right now, okay? Events are in motion and I was sent here to bring you to Lord Haden. That's as far as I know. I'm sorry for what happened to your friends back there, I really am, but I only had the power to take you back, so that's all I did."

Her words calmed Keenth as listened.

"You'll get your answers if, no, when we see him. Seriously, Keenth. Your training days are behind you, so we need to get out of here now before we end up getting caught up in anything."

"No, no I hear you it's just...All this time I've been throwing questions your way, but I never bothered to thank you...So, thank you," Keenth says, bowing.

"Hee hee, you don't need to do all of that. It wasn't a problem at all, really. We'll pull through this, I promise! By the way, welcome to the real world," Cory says as she pulls Keenth up by his arm. "C'mon, let's go!"

"Right!"

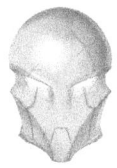

CHAPTER 6

"Jeez, my body feels like it was slammed by a truck," Keenth thinks to himself, before realizing he is in an unfamiliar setting. "W-wait, where in the world am I?"

"Ah, thank goodness you've awakened," an elderly woman answers. "We've been nursing you for the last few days, but I didn't think you would recover as quickly as you did. I'll be sure to let the others know."

"Oh, thanks for keeping an eye on me, I really appreciate it. But that doesn't answer my question about where I am. And you said that you've been nursing me for days...What's been going on lately?"

"You know for a guy who was saved out of the goodness of our hearts, you'd think you would be a bit more grateful," another individual retorts as she walks into the room. "But for the sake of hospitality, this is Azoco. Azoco Village."

Despite never seeing her before, there was a certain air of familiarity with her presence. From what he could tell, Keenth figured that she was roughly his age.

But her long, gracious hair, complimented by her warm, sun-kissed complexion, contrasted with her straightforwardness.

"Azoco? They never said anything about this place at the Academy," Keenth thought out loud. "The last thing I remember was being on the Prospear Bridge and—"

"Ah, so you're one of those. You base everything you know off whatever the Academy or Lantech tells you? I hate to break it to you sweetheart, but that whole Prospear incident happened a week ago."

"It's LanTech–and what did you mean a week ago? Why the hell were you people keeping me cooped up in this hut for so long? I've got to get back to Cory and the others so we can find the Sage! There's no time to waste—"

A frantic Keenth stumbles off of the bed, realizing that his body was in no condition to continue his journey. Trying to get back on his feet, he was approached by a helping hand.

"Alright, alright. Let's just take it easy. Lady Aida and the others did the best they could to keep you alive, but it looks like there's still a long way ahead before you get to play hero, bud. So, do me a favor and keep it together, would you? Your questions will be answered before you know it."

"Okay, fair enough. Thanks, well, again, I guess. By the way, my name is Keenth. Keenth Hedstrom," Keenth responded as he was being helped up. "I take it that it was Lady Aida just now, but you are…?"

"Ah, right. Kendra. Kendra Leight," a young woman acknowledged with a welcoming smile. "Come on, let's get you settled in the village, Keenth."

Stepping out of the hut, Keenth was awestruck by the tangible warmth of the village and its people.

Surrounded by a sea of trees under a drowning blue sky, Azoco was made up of dozens of buildings that were home to its numerous inhabitants.

Everyone from the farmers tending to their crops to the children playing near the forests came out to greet Keenth with open arms. He was further surprised by Kendra presenting him with a wooden bo staff.

"Wow, thanks. I don't know what to say...I really appreciate this gift."

"Don't mention it, Keenth. Don't mention it at all. I'm just glad that you're humbly accepting this gift...this gift of death!"

Kendra suddenly attacked Keenth with a staff of her own. An alarmed Keenth instinctively defended himself, with the villagers surrounding them, eager to see who would come out on top in one-on-one combat.

"Are you out of your mind, lady?? What happened to me getting settled here?" Keenth shouted at the spirited young woman.

"Shut it! I'm doing the talking here! Are you a Lantech spy? A rebel? A vegan??"

"It's LanTech! And I don't know if I should be as confused as I am offended, but could you just give me a minute to catch my breath, lady?"

"The air's for villagers only, you filthy outsider," Kendra counters as she swiftly lands a blow on her unexpecting opponent.

While her pride wouldn't let her say it, she was considerably impressed by how well Keenth was holding up, especially since he was still recovering.

Keenth, realizing that she was holding back from using fatal blows, decided to move from a defensive approach to a surprise attack.

After moving some distance from her, Keenth launched his staff with all of his strength towards Kendra, who was able to easily dodge the weapon.

It penetrated a tree behind her, greatly astonishing her and the other villagers. Using this opportunity, Keenth blitzed his opponent and was able to arm himself with her weapon.

"Give up...You're defenseless!" Keenth says, feeling he himself was running out of stamina. "As fun as all of this is, I don't want to hurt you."

"You? Hurt me? What, is there something about carrying a big stick that goes straight to your head? Are you overcompensating over there buddy or what?" Kendra says to the crowd's amusement.

"You take that back," a clearly flabbergasted Keenth says. "I'm not going to let your petty words get to me, you wench!"

"I mean, by the looks of it, they already are, so–"

"Oh, yeah? Then just take a closer look at this!"

Letting his temper get the best of him, Keenth rapidly spins the staff to gain momentum, before rushing to strike his opponent.

Kendra confidently extends her hand to stop the attack and the sheer force of the clash is enough to cause a massive shockwave throughout the immediate area.

Keenth was blown back and, after getting to his feet once the dust settled, he was surprised to see an unfazed Kendra standing before him. Without words and with little strength left, he was dumbfounded by the villagers' ovation.

"How many times am I going to have to help you up today, man?" Kendra says and sighs as she assists Keenth to his feet.

"Shouldn't be too many as long as you could keep yourself from attacking me again."

"Ha, you'll live," Kendra returned as she swats Keenth's back. "I just had to give the villagers peace of mind by feeling you out. Nothing personal, I promise. So, are we good?"

"Yeah, yeah. We're good…Sore as hell, but good. Now while you're still emotionally stable, could you tell me where I can find my sword? As fun as…whatever this is, I'd feel a lot better having it with me," Keenth responds as he hands Kendra her staff.

"What do we look like, the lost and found? It was one thing to find you floating about, but your sword? Sorry, but consider that long gone, my friend."

"Damn…Sorry, I just…That wasn't just any old sword, but it was from my home village. So much for keeping the legacy alive," Keenth murmurs.

"…I see. Well, we have a lot to cover and you never know when you'll get another surprise death match from me, so why don't you hold onto this for now," Kendra says as she tosses the staff to Keenth. "Consider it a welcoming gift from me to you."

"You know the last time you gave me a staff…"

"Are you still on that? And to be fair, you snatched this from me. So, if you want to be technical…"

"Ahh, fair enough. Thanks again," Keenth says. "If you've got time, I can tell you everything you need to know about me. Sounds alright with you?"

Kendra agreed and the two spent hours upon hours sharing their stories.

From Keenth's time growing up on Colonia Island to Kendra being raised in Azoco Village by Lady Aida, it didn't take long for either of them to realize how much they had in common, despite their different backgrounds.

At this point, it was nightfall and the two were talking over a warm campfire. Although they were practically strangers, there was an undeniable sense of familiarity between the two. Still, Kendra needed to enlighten Keenth about how the world around them works.

"That is quite the series of events, Keenth. So, you're really pressed on finding that Sage, huh? Why not take the opportunity to go back to Colonia?" Kendra asks. "It sounds like your time on the mainland has already had its fair share of twists and turns."

"Truth be told, there's nothing for me back home right now. I really don't see the point of taking a step backwards."

"Really? No parents, siblings, baby mothers? You seem like the deadbeat type—"

"Me? No...Old Man Renzel focused on raising my older brother and I for years."

"You have an older brother? How come you didn't bring him up before?"

"Yeah, his name is Mark. Not much to talk about. He's been gone for about five years now, so..."

"I'm sorry to hear that, Keenth. Was he sick or something?"

"Mark? No, he...Well, it's kind of complicated..."

"Look if you don't want to talk about it, I completely—"

"He drowned while fishing with some of the—"

"Wait, he drowned? Didn't you say you two grew up on islands? How is that even possible?" Kendra blurts.

"I don't know, we never got around to learning how to swim. Like I said, it's complicated."

"I have several questions," Kendra calmly responds. Knowing that it would be better to redirect the conversation, she decided to bring up their sparring session from earlier that afternoon.

"Hey, I don't mean to be that person or whatever, but for someone who handled himself pretty well earlier, why aren't you using your Auraen properly?" Kendra asks. "I mean don't let it go to your head or anything, but, if you put in the effort, you could really make the most of your potential."

"Auraen? They taught us a bit about using Energy back at the Academy, but that's about it. As far as fighting goes, I pretty much follow my gut. It hasn't always worked out for the best, but what can you do, you know?"

"I see. Well, tell you what: you've been on your ass for about a week now, and Mama Kendra's feeling pretty generous. I'll train you up nicely free of charge. Assuming that you don't die or anything, that should bring you up to speed."

"M-mama Kendra? If I die? Look, I appreciate the offer, I really do, but I really need to make my way to Sage Haden. Cory and the others…well, the least I can do is make sure what they did wasn't for nothing."

"Ugh, again with the Sage business. I can't force you or anything, but what's to say you won't run into even more problems once you leave here? Based off of what you've told me, you've been a real magnet for trouble lately. How about this? Give me a few days, about a week tops, to train you up. Sounds straight?"

"That'd work, thanks. Though I have to apologize to you now since I might be a bit of a slow learner. I didn't realize it until my time at the Academy. Would a week still be enough time for us?"

"First thing's first, forget everything you thought you knew up until now. Second, when it comes to training under Mama Kendra, class is always in session. I'm not here to waste our time or anything–for you to really learn about Auraen, you need to allow me to show you firsthand."

Kendra takes a deep breath before being cloaked in a glowing, flowing light-blue Auraen. Even though Keenth felt something similar with Benjamin and the others, he was at a loss for words at the sheer amount of power emitting from her.

Clearly noticing that Keenth is awestruck, Kendra calmly began to explain things in a way he could understand.

"I'm sure you understand by now that this world and everything in it is made of Energy, but its proper name is Auraen. It took some time, but I was able to manifest my Auraen into what I like to call Reiki Mode. Through meditation, my spirit shines through, bringing my strength, speed, and senses to their peak."

"This…no…you are incredible, Kendra…Simply incredible. Is this something you can teach me in a week or would I need more time with you?"

"I guess that remains to be seen, grasshopper. While everyone has Auraen, I believe that roughly one in five could utilize their own properly. Even then, there's no guarantee what, if anything, would manifest in your case," Kendra says as she releases herself from Reiki Mode.

"Just to put things in perspective, I am the only person in the Azoco with this ability."

"Really? Out of the whole village? You could have fooled me, Kendra."

"That's understandable. You see Azoco is a place where people with exceptional Auraen potential find refuge. The world could be a pretty dark place and I'm glad Aida and the others were able to make a place where people like us could call home."

"Ha, that Mama Kendra business makes sense now that I think about it. But, anyway, is it alright if I could get some rest? Something tells me that I'll definitely be needing it."

"Color me surprised: you aren't as dumb as you look. We have a cot laid out for you not too far from my hut. And don't get any ideas! After all, I'm not a first date kind of girl," Kendra jokes.

"Kendra Victoria Leight!! You watch that tone of yours right now," Lady Aida shouts as she makes her way toward them.

"Y-yes, Ma'am. Go on, and get out of here, Keenth. We start at 5AM sharp. Be sure to drink plenty of water," Kendra states.

As Keenth wandered off, Kendra got Lady Aida up to speed on the young man and her plans for him moving forward. While she may come off as a bit too stern at times, Kendra always confided in Lady Aida as if she was her own mother.

While Keenth's arrival felt like a stroke of fate, there was an odd sense of foreboding between the two women.

"Why the long face, Kendra? I haven't seen you this concerned since you found out that chocolate milk didn't come from brown cows," Lady Aida said to lighten the mood.

"Well, for one, that's debatable. But in all seriousness, I don't know. I just can't put my finger on it, but there's something different about this one."

"I'm not big on coincidences," Kendra continues. "But there has to be a reason why he ended up with us the way he did. I can't shake that feeling, you know?"

"Ah, so the infamous Mama Kendra has a heart after all. I'm kidding...Especially since that would make me Auntie Aida. But don't stress yourself about it too much. We'll cross that bridge when we get there, young lady."

"I guess, you're right. I told him that I'd be able to train him in a week. Do you think that'll be enough time?"

"Well, you probably shouldn't make deadlines like that without thinking them through. Why a week, though?"

"He keeps going on and on about meeting up with Haden. Who am I to hold someone that determined back?"

"I see. Well, we'll see how things turn out soon enough. Let's call it a night, dear."

Keeping to her word, Kendra gave Keenth a day to rest while she made training preparations. In that time, Keenth took in the sights and had the opportunity to formally meet more of the other villagers.

Most of the younger children were amazed at Keenth's recent adventures and sharing those stories from Colonia and the Training Academy gave him the chance to reflect on how much he had gone through.

While it was humbling to remember his past, Keenth took great pride in being in such a welcoming environment, especially since Kendra shared how many of the villagers had so much in common with Keenth and his upbringing.

Lady Aida observed the camaraderie and thought to herself about how Keenth being there was the most welcoming surprise that they had in some time.

"Keenth, was it? Let's see what Larkin's son brings to the table," Lady Aida thinks to herself.

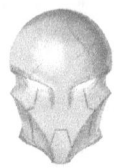

CHAPTER 7

Finally, the day of training was upon them. Keenth was awoken by a bucket of freezing water at around 4AM. While he was somewhat frustrated at this, Kendra claimed the bucket slipped and that a morning run around the village would be a great way to dry off.

Irritated yet competitive, Keenth made it a point to put his best effort into this training. He believed that time on the islands had prepared him for whatever Kendra would throw his way.

It took quite a bit of effort, but he was at least able to keep up with his newfound mentor. Mildly impressed, Kendra told him to take a few minutes before they began their actual warm-up. With his soul somewhat crushed, a visibly exhausted Keenth nodded his head to show he was ready to get to work.

Kendra smiled and told Keenth to ready himself before she charged forward. Even though he was ready, he was surprised at her instantly tapping into Reiki Mode.

Before he could react, Kendra struck him from behind with enough force to send him flying into a nearby lake. Before he could fall into the water, Kendra repeated this attack to redirect him back to land.

"I suggest you take the time here in Azoco to learn how to swim," she shouts.

Keenth was upset at having to train like this while still not fully recovered, but Kendra insisted that if he could push himself enough to stand toe to toe with her in her empowered state, then he'd be stronger than he could ever imagine.

Inspired, Keenth rushed at her once again, but was swatted into the lake for a second time. Only this time, Kendra refused to save him. Instead, she instructed him to run laps around the village to dry off and try again.

It took several times for him to realize Kendra was slowly rebuilding his stamina and strengthening him to improve. With this fresh motivation, Keenth continued to press on.

As the week went on, Keenth and Kendra were hard at work and the villagers noticed. They gave them their space as expected, but couldn't help but admire the amount of effort being put into training.

Keenth was surprisingly running at a pace that was comparable to Kendra's, though she would say she was holding back.

On the fifth day, Keenth was finally able to spar without being tossed into the water. To his surprise, Kendra offered a congratulatory fist bump.

"Congrats, kiddo. We're finished here," Kendra says, wiping her forehead. "It took some work, but you've done made Mama proud."

"R-really? I feel like I could barely get you to show me what you're really capable of," Keenth replies. "Though you won't find any complaints from me!"

"Yeah, yeah, well, just be glad you haven't seen my bad side...yet!

Anyway, Aida and the others prepared a huge meal to commemorate you coming out in one piece. Go ahead and clean up so we can grab some of our greatest home-cooked meals!"

Keenth and Kendra joined the villagers for amazing food, toasts, and laughs which carried on throughout the night. There was a tangible sense of pride in the improvements Keenth had made in such a short period of time, with many agreeing that he had a wealth of untapped potential.

Despite this, Keenth humbly downplayed the fact that he hadn't unlocked any particular new abilities under Kendra's tutelage.

He was reassured that certain things take time though and knew that he should hold his head up high over the results of his hard work so far.

When asked what he planned to do next, he commented that he was too stuffed and exhausted to think straight, but would have an answer in a few days.

Little did Keenth know that the final part of his training meant allowing his body to recover.

As the villagers made their ways home, Kendra approached an unexpecting Keenth with a particular proposition. She told him to follow her into the forest and he silently agreed.

After quietly making their way through miles of woods, Kendra and Keenth finally reached their destination.

Keenth looked on as Kendra prepared torches to help them navigate through a nearby hidden cavern.

Once inside, Keenth was surprised to see a small group of villagers waiting for them.

"Took you long enough," a young man says, grunting as he sharpens his spear. "I figured you of all people would have a problem if anyone showed up late."

"Ah, shut it, dummy. You all knew I was bringing Keenth over and I didn't want to risk any of the others trailing us," Kendra replies. "That said, thanks for holding things down in the meantime, Richard."

Keenth was shocked that Kendra could casually talk to such a physically imposing young man such as Richard.

On top of that, none of the others in attendance seemed all too surprised by it.

Seeing various weapons scattered alongside dozens of books around the room, Keenth could barely hide his confusion.

"What? You act like you've never seen a library before? Richard's the name! Nice to meet you," he says kindly. "Go ahead and grab a seat, bro. We've got a ton to talk about, now that you two are here."

"Ah, right. Keenth, Richard. Richard, Keenth. This freeloader comes in and out of Azoco without much notice, so that's why you didn't meet him until now. What else, what else…Oh, that old crab over there is Weiss. He found you and brought you to safety, so be sure to thank him," Kendra says as she sits on the edge of the table where everyone was gathered.

"Seriously? Thank you, Sir. By any chance, was there anyone else that you saved or…"

"Sorry son, but you were the only one that I was able to bring back," Weiss quietly responds. "The fact that we found you alive was nothing short of a miracle."

Keenth nodded in understanding as Kendra continued on. Richard and the others made up a committee of sorts that supported the village from behind the scenes.

Being more in touch with the events surrounding Tortuga and

the rest of Hasania gave this group the opportunity to do the best for Azoco within their means.

It was obvious that while Lady Aida was seen as the respected figurehead of the village, but Kendra was obviously the face of this faction. Keenth was particularly attentive when the conversation was redirected on the events that took place on the Prospear Bridge.

"I normally keep Azoco away from what goes on in Tortuga, but once I sensed what was going on, I reached out to Richard as soon as I could," Kendra explains. "There was something so bizarre with what was going on. Keenth, I remember what you told me about how you and the others were fighting. But looking back then, I couldn't get a sense of who you were up against..."

Confused, Keenth thought back on the events leading up to him arriving in Azoco Village. In his mind, there was no doubt that he was definitely clashing with hostile opponents between the attacks on Training Academy and the Prospear Bridge.

From there, Richard took the opportunity to explain things from his perspective.

"Believe it or not, you fought alongside a few warriors that I knew, Keenth. I doubt you had the opportunity to have formal introductions, but by the time I made it the bridge..." Richard began. "Look we're not bringing this up for the sake of talking in circles, but don't feel as if you are alone in this."

"What do you mean? Weiss said I was the only one that he found, remember?"

"Right, but he found you days after the battle. How do you suppose you made it off the bridge anyway?"

"Hmm...It's a bit foggy," Keenth says as he thinks back. "The last thing I remember is when I was telling Benjamin and the others that—"

"Wait, Benjamin? As in Benjamin Palorro? You fought alongside him??" Richard exclaims.

"Um, yeah that's his name. Young guy? Has a thing for fire? Do you know him?" Keenth says, surprised.

"It's Efir! And know him? I helped train the guy!" Richard proudly shouts. "You have nothing to worry about, Keenth. If you fought along with him, then I'm sure that he and the others are fine!"

"Seriously? That's amazing," Keenth says, relieved. "I…Well, we need to go find them then, don't we?"

"We're sure they're all fine for now, Keenth. But that's not what we brought you here to talk about," Kendra says. "There's something we need you to confirm. Take a look at this and let us know if it looks familiar."

Keenth made his way to a slab Kendra was pointing at, only to be horrified at what he was seeing: A fully armored warrior from the attacks on the Academy and the Prospear Bridge.

"Don't worry, it won't attack," Kendra assures Keenth as she approaches.

"More specifically, your reaction confirmed everything that we needed to know. Look closely, Keenth. This is completely mechanical… You and the others were up against machines the whole time."

"How is that even possible? The way they fought. The way they reacted. Sorry, but there has to be a mistake; there's no way that they were machines, Kendra."

"Think about it. You told me about the attack on the Academy and how they were unfazed by everything. I mean sure, you could brush it off like they were wearing masks or something, I'll give you that. But how do you explain how their leader on the bridge shrugged off your attacks like they were nothing?"

Keenth was at a loss for words as Richard went on to explain their findings. There were not many clues of substance after LanTech and the local authorities closed off the surrounding area, but there was something especially peculiar about this armor.

"Word around the way is that their primary means of attacking is through explosives. Call it simple, but people refer to these things as Bombers," Richard reveals. "Keenth, what makes this thing a cut above the rest is that its self-destruction mechanism was somehow disabled during your bout on the bridge."

"Disabled how? We were pretty much fighting an uphill battle the whole time," Keenth asks. "Maybe there's another explanation for this?"

"No, trust me, I went through this machine myself and noticed that its sensors were frozen solid. The ice was so impressive that it took my Efir abilities to thaw it out properly," Richard assures.

"Oh...That's it! It must've been Beth! She definitely had the ability to do something like that," a Keenth exclaims.

"Well, Keenth, it sounds like you had quite the crew to fight alongside," Kendra says with a supportive smile. "Look, I know that this was a lot to throw on you in one night, but thanks for your help in figuring this out. Knowing this changes everything. I'll bring you out here in a few days again, once you are well-rested."

Keenth was a bit taken back by Kendra's decision to end the meeting the way she did. Though he didn't ask out loud, she eventually explained herself to Keenth on their way back to the village.

"I'm sure there is a lot for you to process right now, Keenth. I don't want to force anything on you. We're just trying to see what's best for our village before the issue with the Bombers affects Azoco. You understand, don't you?"

"Actually, I don't. If there are people as powerful as you and the others, why aren't you out there trying to stop the Bombers now? Don't you care that people are getting killed out there?"

"We cared enough to take you in, didn't we? Look, you may not get it, but we have to be smart about our abilities. There is no telling what's out there and the last thing we need is to draw attention to ourselves. LanTech and most of the warriors keep their noses out of Azoco and I want it to stay that way."

"I get it. I would be doing the same if we were back in Colonia. Sorry for speaking out of line, Kendra."

"That's Mama Kendra. And it's fine. Speaking of Colonia, I have to ask you again. What do you plan to do from here? Are you sure you don't want to head back there, or are you really sure about handling that Sage Haden business you told me about?"

"I'm not sure. I think I'll need some time to think about it. Like you said, this is a lot to take in."

"I get you. Look, just get your rest, and we'll figure it out, Keenth."

So Keenth took the time to rest up, and for quite a bit too. Three days later, Keenth starts his day, this time not flinching at cold water splashing him first thing in the morning. Instead, the sound of rain slowly brought him back to reality.

At first Keenth thought it was a bit strange because it hadn't rained at all since he'd been in the village, but he didn't dwell on it too much. Instead, he made his rounds before being greeted by a group of villagers.

The time had come for Keenth to make his decision. With a heavy heart, he informed them that he would be continuing his journey to Sage Haden.

Though bittersweet, many understood where he was coming from. Keenth thanked them for everything and promised he would return as soon as possible. With that, Lady Aida presented Keenth with a valuable treasure that left him speechless.

"Is this my sword? But how? I thought it was lost at Prospear Bridge."

"Well, we thought so too, but Mr. Weiss and the others went back and didn't leave a stone unturned until they found it for you," Aida explains. "After all, we wouldn't want you showing up to a Sage looking out of place or anything."

"Wow, I can't thank you all enough for everything you've done for me. To be honest, I don't know what to expect, but I feel much more confident, thanks to my time here."

"Don't mention it, man. The pleasure was all ours," Kendra replies, stretching her arms and letting out a yawn to the humor some of the villagers. "Give the Sage our best and just be sure to bring me back a shot glass on your way back!"

"Absolutely. Don't you mention it," Keenth exclaimed. "Actually, before I head out, Kendra, I—"

Before he could finish, a massive foreboding Auraen was felt not too far from the village. Aida commented on this to Kendra and the decision was made for the villagers to seek refuge in their respective homes.

Kendra asked Aida to keep an eye on the village while she went ahead to see things with her own eyes. Keenth, however, surprised them with the fact that he was able to sense all of this as well.

"I can feel it too...It's a few miles outside of the village. If I head over now, that could buy you guys some time in case things go south," Keenth says, drawing his sword.

"Are you crazy? You've improved, sure, but you have no idea what's out there. This is something for us to handle," Kendra protests. "We appreciate it, but this isn't the first time that people have come our way looking for trouble."

"I know, Kendra, I know. But there's something familiar about this Auraen. I can't quite put my finger on it, but it feels like I've felt this before. Besides, I was leaving anyway and they're technically out of the village, so it's all fair game."

Before Kendra could continue to go back and forth with Keenth, Lady Aida gave him their blessing to go ahead.

She told Kendra to have faith in Keenth and, as the leader of Azoco, it was her responsibility to protect the village and its people.

"Well, don't do anything I wouldn't do," Kendra says, extending her arm for a fist bump, only to be surprised by Keenth hugging her.

"Hey, hey! We're not there yet, so don't get all sentimental on me now."

"Don't worry. I learned a few things that'll make you proud," Keenth says as he departs.

With that, Keenth raced towards the outskirts of the village in an attempt to thwart the potential threats ahead. As he pressed forward, there was an undeniable sense of familiarity that could be felt down to his core.

Memories of his time at the Training Academy and his journey to the Sage came flooding in as Keenth moved forward until he noticed an uneasy fog covering the surrounding area.

The further he progressed, the more difficult it was for him to see ahead. It was around that time he heard a voice calling out to him.

"It's funny who you randomly run into these days," a mysterious voice states. "I would complain about the rain, but it's my fault for not bringing an umbrella."

"That voice," Keenth thought to himself. "You're—"

"Agent Fallon: James Fallon. It's been quite a while, kid. What's new?" Agent Fallon says as he slowly emerges from the fog.

"Can't complain. Is there something I can help you with, Agent?"

"Help me? Maybe the news is slow to come out around here, but things have really gone to hell lately. If anything, I came all the way out here to help you, young man," Agent Fallon sarcastically replies.

"If you're talking about what happened at the Training Academy, thanks for your concern. But as you can see, I'm doing just fine. I'll ask again a bit clearer: what do you want?" Keenth asks sternly.

"A bit moody today, are we? Well, since you insist, let's talk. The incident at the Academy changed everything. We thought just about everyone didn't make it out of there alive, but clearly you were fortunate enough to live another day."

"Wait, what do you mean just about everyone?"

"Hey, now, the grown-up's talking. From there, there was a little scene caused out on the Prospear Bridge not too long later. We looked into it and thought there wouldn't be many survivors. But look at the stars, it turns out that you were not only an active participant in the skirmish, but was left unscathed as well."

The tension increased as Keenth tried his best to maintain his composure. The forbidding fog slowly began to clear and Agent Fallon took a few steps forward. Keenth, renewed with the confidence afforded to him thanks to his training, moved forward as well.

"I would really appreciate it if you got to the point, Fallon."

"Hey, you've got some nerve. I'll give you that. But let's quit the games. You are a LanTech trainee who failed to account for yourself, despite our efforts to ensure your well-being. Conversely, you've allied yourself with rebels and were involved in an incident that left several people dead and even more critically injured," Agent Fallon sternly stated. "The fact of the matter is that you or your little friends out there have something that belongs to me. Something, as you probably understand, I can't exactly leave unattended."

"So, allow me to make things clear for you: Keenth Hedstrom, you are a person of interest. Now, drop your weapon or I will have to use aggressive measures to apprehend you." Agent Fallon drew his sword.

Sensing Agent Fallon's Auraen sharpening, Keenth firmly held his ground, with his sword directed squarely at the LanTech Agent.

Resolve reflected in his eyes as he felt how his training had prepared him specifically for this moment.

"Pretty bold to draw a weapon at a LanTech Official," Agent Fallon says.

"Well it wouldn't be the first time," Keenth defiantly stated. "After all, I'm just defending myself from someone behind the Bomber attacks as far as I can tell."

"Really, now? Wow. To think you would go and say all of that. Now that I think about it, the two of us did have a little session at the Academy, didn't we? How about you show me if you learned any new tricks," Fallon said, signaling for Keenth to make his move.

Tightening his grip on his sword, Keenth's Auraen wildly roared throughout the area, which was enough to even impress Agent Fallon.

"Well, would you look at that? I guess you aren't all talk, after all. If I didn't know any better, I'd say you're fixing to kill me dead right here and now!"

Knowing that the time for words was over, Keenth rushed towards Agent Fallon. His opponent was seemingly caught off guard, seeing how he did not even have the opportunity to properly ready his sword to defend himself.

As Keenth swiftly struck his blade down, he was surprised to see that his attack was blocked.

Agent Fallon had an arrogant smirk on his face as Keenth realized that there was someone between the two of them.

The dark black blade that blocked Keenth's sword was eerily familiar. As he focused, he came to the soul crushing realization of who was ahead.

"...Paul?"

CHAPTER 8

As the rain continued to pour down in the forest, Keenth distanced himself in an attempt to comprehend this turn of events.

Since he finds himself at a loss for words, Agent Fallon takes the opportunity to address what was at hand.

"What seems to be the problem? You aren't so chatty all of a sudden," Agent Fallon states. "If I didn't know any better, I would think that you just saw a ghost or something."

"P-Paul...But how?" an astonished Keenth asks. "You...I thought with what happened at the Academy that you..."

"Really? You really cared about who was left behind at the Academy? You definitely could've fooled me by the way you went off on your own program. But, hey, no worries, consider it water under the bridge," Agent Fallon says as he draws his sword to Keenth's surprise.

After carefully looking him over, Keenth noticed that Paul was armed with an intricate metal brace over his upper right arm and a bright silver band around his head which seemingly was the cause of the spiritless expression in his eyes.

"Fallon, you bastard! Just what the hell did you do to my friend?" Keenth demands, trying his best to keep himself under control. "Why would Paul be aligned with someone like you of all people?"

"Well, for one, I'm the one who saved your so-called friend. If anything, you should be thanking me," Agent Fallon answered as he approached Paul. "Most of the others in your Academy weren't as lucky as—"

"Yo, Jimmy, how long are ya gonna keep yapping for?" an unknown voice interrupts. "You're not exactly paying us for overtime, ya know!"

"Yeah, yeah…Just quit your whining, Claude," Agent Fallon snaps. "Better yet, how about you do us all a favor and choke on a salad or something."

The rude, obscene Claude was a thuggish, unkempt, and an overall sloppy excuse for an adult, so Agent Fallon's attitude towards him was somewhat justified.

Still, Keenth couldn't understand why any LanTech Agent would ally himself with such an individual.

"You know what? I'm out! You ain't worth the stress, kid. This can't be good for my heart," Claude scoffs as he tried to use rain to clean off a stain on his shirt to no avail.

"Oh, so suggesting a salad is bad for you, but stuffing your stomachs, yes, plural, with raw pork shoulder isn't? Champ, you've gotta explain that logic for me," Agent Fallon mocks.

Before he could continue though, another individual got serious.

"Fallon, Claude…I could care less about what you two are going on about, but quit wasting so much goddamn time. Since you got the blond kid right in front of you, the only thing left is to retrieve the machine. Come on, Claude. We're heading to the village."

This young woman was the opposite of Claude in every way imaginable: tall, lean, and all business. Agent Fallon quietly nodded in agreement as Claude made confirmations with a small tracking device.

"Don't get so pushy, Kusari. Finding the mech should be no problem," Claude says while his device begins to rapidly beep.

"And just like that, we're in there! A few miles ahead, right where the runt came from."

"H-Hey! Where do you think you are going? There is nothing for you back there," Keenth protests.

"Fallon, call these guys off right now!"

"Good work, Claude. Remember that I'll be there to clear out any potential opposition. That way, you should be able to do whatever you have to do without any issues," Kusari responds, standing behind a shocked Keenth.

"How the hell did she get past me so quickly?" Keenth thinks to himself.

"More importantly, her Auraen is ridiculously off the charts. She might even be—"

"Oi! Wait up for me," Claude pleads as he feverishly jogs in Kusari's direction.

Keenth attempts to stop the two individuals, only to be thwarted by a sudden attack from Paul.

Torn between the situation in front of him and the oncoming threat to Azoco, Keenth's agitation rises.

"Fallon, I don't have time for this!" Keenth yells while gritting his teeth. "Stop whatever you are doing to Paul right now, or I'll—"

"Or you'll what," Paul replies. "You heard Agent Fallon. Now put down your weapon or you will leave me no choice but to use deadly force on you. Don't let it get to the point where I have to make the choice for you, Hedstrom."

Keenth is speechless at the fact that Paul is seemingly attacking on his own accord. A smug smile crosses Agent Fallon's face.

"I don't know about you, but it sounds to me like your old buddy isn't kidding around," Agent Fallon announced.

"Do you understand now? Hopefully so, because like Kusari said, we can't afford to be wasting so much gosh darn time."

While Keenth is dealing with this dilemma, a clearly winded Claude finds his way to Azoco Village.

While most would not be able to find this mysterious refuge under normal circumstances, Claude Young's mechanical engineering background proves to be quite advantageous.

"Bastards…I'll never forgive them for making me rush all the way out here like this," Claude moans as he makes his way through the seemingly uninhabited village.

"My radar can't pinpoint that mech anymore than it already has, so now I gotta check the entire stupid dump. Man, I tell ya, I don't get paid enough for this stuff. Overworked and underappreciated…Story of my life."

"You know, if you need a place to stay, I could show you where our farms are. You would fit right in with some of our slower pigs," Kendra announces as she approached Claude. "So, tell me, just what the hell are you doing in my village?"

"Add disrespected to that list," Claude snarls. "You would think that someone like me, Claude the Great, would be known even out here like this sorry—"

Before he can continue any further, Claude is slapped down to the ground.

Attempting to catch Kendra by surprise with a hidden knife, he is immediately kicked across the face, landing head first into the muddy turf.

"OKAY!! I-I'm just here on a job for Fallon's mech! That's all, I'm serious! Please, please, please! I don't want the smoke," Claude begs. "I'll tell you anything, just please stop with the face! It's all I've got going for me!"

"Fallon," Kendra thought out loud, remembering that Keenth had brought him up previously. "Are you talking about the Agent? Why the hell would someone from LanTech be working with someone like you?"

"LanTech? Please! As if I would be caught dead working with any of them! This is strictly off the books! I'm just here to grab the Bomber and I'll be out of your hair. Now if you'd be a good little girl and—"

Catching a swift knee to the face, Claude is rendered unconscious, while Kendra tries to put this information together.

Sensing Keenth's fight outside the village, she begins to make her way to help when a foreign voice calls out to her.

"Do you really think it's a good idea to leave your little village unattended?" Kusari asks. "Not that I care either way, but even Claude would agree that it is probably something you should take into consideration."

"I guess when it rains, it pours. I take it that you're from the same team as pug face," Kendra replies, while trying to figure out how she wasn't able to sense her sooner.

"Do yourself a favor and take that trash out with you back to wherever you came from."

"Sorry, but that's out of the question. A job's a job and I'm here to make sure that no one intervenes with what we're set out to do. The name's Kusari, by the way. And you?"

"There's no need for you to know. I'm going to make short work of you and deal with that Fallon guy myself. No one comes to my village looking to start trouble without having to deal with the consequences," Kendra says as she adopts a battle stance.

"Sorry if I gave you the wrong impression, but me speaking on Claude's behalf is strictly a professional courtesy. Anyway, why are you so up in arms about us retrieving something that does not belong to you in the first place?"

"Fair point. Why does Fallon want that mech back so badly? If it was such a priority, he would be going at it with full support through the Empire. What's the reason for doing things off the grid?"

"Beats me, kid. Nothing personal, but I'm a stickler for timeliness and we've wasted enough time already. One way or another, we're going to get that machine."

"Over my dead body," Kendra says, launching herself toward her opponent.

The impact of Kendra's attack on Kusari could have easily been confused as distant thunder which accompanied the unrelenting rain in the area.

This took Kendra by surprise because an attack of this magnitude had been known to easily break mountainsides.

Alternately despite her tall stature, Kusari's combat style was deceptively fluid as she was able to keep up the pace with Kendra's unrelenting blows.

Kusari was clearly focused on defeating Kendra, while Kendra's mind wavered slightly due to Keenth's situation.

"First, you refuse to tell me your name," Kusari states. "But now you won't give it your all against me? Wouldn't you agree that you're being a bit unpleasant?"

"Keep your thoughts to yourself," Kendra says, but realizing that Kusari is absolutely correct. "The sooner I deal with you, the better."

"You're worried about him, aren't you? Interesting…It's as if you don't respect his abilities as a warrior enough in its own right. If that's where your mind is at, then at this rate, he'll probably—"

Kendra swiftly punches her opponent, which knocks Kusari a few feet back. Smiling and wiping a small trickle of blood from her lips, Kusari draws large daggers with each hand and begins her counterattack.

Reaching out with her right arm, Kendra's battle staff flies into her grasp as Kusari rushes toward her.

Kusari attacks though without giving her opponent any opportunity to retaliate.

Still, Kendra is able to effectively block each successive assault while preparing to shift the battle in her favor.

"You know, for someone with your abilities, it's a damn shame that you aren't using them for good," Kendra says, while blocking an elbow from Kusari.

"Maybe, under different circumstances, someone like you would—"

"Just save it, you ignorant girl. The last thing that I have time for is to hear ramblings from someone who doesn't have the slightest clue of how the world really works. Unlike your perfect little village, the real world is far from all sunshine and rainbows."

"Azoco is far from perfect, but that doesn't stop us from choosing to live our lives to better one another. How do you look at yourself in the mirror knowing that you allow your strength to be used by whoever is willing to pay the highest? How do you even sleep at night?"

"That's the naïve mindset that I'm talking about. You and your people have the freedom to choose what you do. Meanwhile, the rest of us are living day by day and so have to use our abilities to survive. The only choice we can make is between life and death."

Kusari's statement clearly struck a chord and it gave her the opportunity to slash Kendra across the right side of her face.

Now with a few feet of distance between one another, Kusari decided to cut their conversation short and complete the task at hand.

"Between LanTech and the fighting we do among ourselves, did you really think someone like you would have a chance against me? While you live peacefully tucked away from everything that's going on, I live in cold, hard reality every single day. You asked how I sleep at night? When you're living a life like mine, you don't even have that luxury."

"Stop making excuses for the actions that you've taken," Kendra says as she wipes the blood from her face. "And I could give a damn about what you think of me or the others here, but the moment that you decided to step foot in my village, you've become an issue that I have to deal with."

"Tell me something…Do you really think I didn't know about this village before this job?" Kusari replies. "If so, it goes beyond naïvety at this point. That would just be full-blown arrogance."

"What are you talking about?"

"Just because we didn't approach Azoco before, doesn't mean we are unaware of its existence. Did you think I couldn't tell? After all, it's obvious that there is some sort of ability that causes an illusion of this being an endless forest to most people looking in from the outside."

"But here is something you all didn't take into consideration.

Auraen abilities are only as effective as their users," Kusari continues. "Put simply, an illusion technique from people like you wouldn't affect someone like me because my strength is on a completely higher level."

"You seem pretty sure of yourself," Kendra says, preparing to engage her opponent again. "Don't act as if our fight is already over, Kusari."

"You really don't seem to understand. From what I can tell, you are the only warrior here with capabilities that could even come close to mine. Even then, this little fight has pretty much been over even before it started."

"I am the only warrior here," Kendra thinks to herself. After coming to a crucial realization, she decided it was time to finally put an end to their bout. "Kendra. Kendra Leight..."

"Hmm? Why are you saying that all of a sudden?"

"Believe it or not, you made a few interesting points. With that in mind, I wouldn't be much of a person I didn't tell you my name."

"Really now and why's that?"

"That's because it would be a shame not to know the name of the person who takes your life," Kendra replies as the ground below her begins to tremble.

"What the hell is this? What are you doing?"

"Something that I should have done since the beginning. While I will admit you made a few interesting points earlier, there's something in particular that I completely disagree with."

"And just what's that?" Kusari asks as the pressure of Kendra's Auraen continues to increase.

"The audacity to think that your strength could compare to Azoco's finest!"

Kendra's Auraen erupts as raging light-blue waves of energy

vibrantly surround Kusari. Kendra then slams her staff into the ground below her and completely overpowers Kusari with a swift punch to the stomach.

Before Kusari can even comprehend what was going on, she releases a series of brutal punches to her opponent's face, each successive blow causing visible shockwaves throughout the village.

Kusari desperately retaliates by trying to stab Kendra with one of her daggers, only for the Azoco Warrior to immediately stop her by mercilessly snapping Kusari's wrist.

Screaming in agony, Kusari is met with a quick backhand from her opponent, before being thrown forward by a palm thrust from Kendra.

It was clear that Kendra's strength and speed had increased multiple times over.

Still the real cause for concern was that for the first time in years, Kusari found herself completely and utterly dominated. Speechless at this realization, Kusari stands shocked as Kendra sternly speaks out to her.

"I guess now's the best time to thank you, Kusari."

"Thank me? Is this some kind of sick joke?"

"No, seriously. For the first time in a while, I'm finally using my powers for their true purpose: to defend my village. I was recently using my abilities to help Keenth get to where he needs to be, but it is a different case when it comes to fighting you."

"As if that reasoning is enough," Kusari retorts. "I'm not someone who will simply go away over something like this. Not that I'll give you the chance to, but if you want to stop me, you'll have to kill me."

"If that's the case, then so be it. If it comes between that and losing the people I love, then the choice is simple. You've made your decisions, now live with them," Kendra states and raises her left arm, while her right arm supports it.

The entire village shakes with the overwhelming amount of energy that Kendra is conjuring. Kusari is shocked to realize she cannot move.

The sheer force of Kendra's power causes her to fall on one knee as a massive wave of Auraen obliterates everything in its direction.

As a large cloud of dust and smoke appears, Kendra slowly closes her eyes and solemnly considers what she's done.

"You did what you had to do, Kendra. Move ahead, move forward," she thinks to herself, while bringing her Auraen levels down to focus on her breathing.

"If I'm right about this, Keenth should be okay against his current opponent. Still, there's no telling what Fallon has under his sleeve. If I leave now, I should be able to—"

Kendra is abruptly stopped when several large needles pierce her right shoulder. Before she can remove them, a massive explosion erupts where she attacked Kusari. An obscenely powerful Auraen emerges, as Kendra realizes what is happening.

"I stand corrected, Kendra. You are more powerful than I gave you credit for," Kusari states as the wild smoke clears. "But I can't stress enough that my strength is beyond your understanding."

The needles rip from Kendra's body, back into the ominous clouds surrounding her opponent. Preparing to finish her bout with Kusari, Kendra is shocked to see her Reiki Mode dissipate.

"M-My powers...What did you do?"

"Me? You decided to show your true power and I simply did the same. Though, unfortunately for you, you'll find that my style of handling things isn't nearly as forgiving as yours."

Kendra distanced herself and rearmed her staff. With the smoke finally cleared, she saw how powerful Kusari had become. Her robes were now adorned with countless large needles which matched the makeshift crown on her head.

"Divine Willow Fang. I don't believe you told me the proper name for what you used against me earlier, but the least I could do is tell you what you are up against, Kendra."

Kendra feels speechless at Kusari's drastic change. Even without actively attacking, the waves of Kusari's Auraen raise the tension to even greater levels.

Even though Kendra was truly recognized as the most powerful warrior in Azoco, she knew deep down she did not know how this fight would end.

Kendra moves in to attack, but Kusari easily dodges her and she realizes that her foe has effortlessly made her way back to the village when she raises her arm to signify her final point.

"Before I end this, I guess now would be the best time to thank you in return. After all, when I get the call, I'm strictly business when it comes to the task. But I've decided that what I'm about to do this little village of yours will be quite enjoyable."

"Like I said earlier…Over my dead body," Kendra retorts, her eyes focused on her opponent.

"I guess it's settled," Kusari replies as she snapped her wrist back into place.

"Keenth, you need to hold out just a little longer. It looks like my hands will be tied for a bit," Kendra thought to herself. "My full focus needs to be on this girl and her alone."

"Kendra Leight! The time for talking is over," Kusari announces as the Auraen needles that she summoned methodically swirl around her. "Now, allow me to show you how to kill someone properly."

"Hey, man, you call that a swing? My grandma could do better than that!"

"Just what the hell is your grandma doing with a sword at her age, Paul?"

"Focus, Keenth! If you're such a great swordsman, so go ahead and prove it!"

"Ha, be careful what you ask for! Now, get ready, because I won't hold back!"

"Good! I wouldn't expect any less. Let's go!"

The sound of blades distantly clashing in the forest brings Keenth back to reality as his fight with Paul continues.

After attempts at reaching out to Paul were met with failure, Keenth decides to apply the skills that were recently sharpened during his training in Azoco.

"You're definitely Paul...There's no mistaking it," Keenth comments, shocked at how his opponent was easily able to keep up with his pace and meticulously apply pressure in return. "But I still can't believe that you got this powerful in such a short amount of time."

"It is nothing for someone like you to understand, Hedstrom. The only thing for you to do is to stay in your place," Paul responds, while swinging his sword.

Keenth parries the attack, only for Paul to attack him twice with his knee. Keenth grabs his side to confirm that those hits were enough to bruise a couple of his ribs.

The instant he looks up, Paul lunges forward and slams Keenth's head into a nearby tree trunk.

Falling to one knee, Keenth's head is held up by his hair as Paul readies his sword to impale him between the eyes. Without a moment to lose, Keenth drives his sword through Paul's stomach.

With regret in his eyes, Keenth pulls back, but is horrified at seeing Paul completely unaffected. In response, Paul discards his sword to use both hands to effortlessly lift Keenth by the neck, aiming to choke the life out of him.

"Don't get so cocky," Keenth shouts as he sharpened his Auraen, giving him the opportunity to free himself.

"Upgrades or not, you're a thousand years away from my level," Keenth says as he savagely headbutts Paul. He follows this up by striking Paul across the face. Catching his breath, Keenth quickly retrieves both of their swords. "Now where were we," Keenth proclaims, while tossing Paul's weapon toward him, continuing their fight. "If words won't bring you back, then I'll just have to beat the hell out of you until they do."

"Don't get too full of yourself," Paul says as he raises his sword. "I wouldn't expect any less from you. Don't expect that to happen again, Keenth. Let's go!"

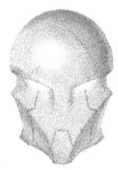

CHAPTER 9

"What did you just say, Paul?"

"You heard me, Keenth! Don't act like you're stupid all of a sudden. Now let's wrap this up or else Aamina will tear us up for not being ready for the Keyes Ceremony in the morning."

"Aamina? Keyes Ceremony? That was almost a month ago," Keenth thought to himself. "What in the world is going through his head right now?"

"Well, if you're just going to stand around like that, then I'll make my move. You should know by now that sword of yours stands no chance against my Fehrenblade," Paul states as he readies his stance.

"Time to end this...Wait, w-what the hell? What's on my arm?"

Paul was shocked at the sight of the metallic brace on his right arm and Keenth was equally confused. Keenth moved forward in an attempt to calm Paul.

"Get back...Just get the hell away from me," Paul demands. "I...I just need to get to the bottom of this. Just give me a goddamn second to focus."

Placing his hand on his forehead to help himself concentrate, Paul screams out in pain as the silver band across his head releases a series of violent electric currents throughout his body.

Without a moment of hesitation, Keenth tosses his sword aside and rushes over to help. Paul, who is writhing on the ground, struggles to plead for his friend to assist him.

"K-Keenth...P-please..."

"Man, what a damn waste."

"Fallon! What the hell is happening? What's going on with Paul?"

"Back when that situation was going on at the Academy, I took your friend here in for a few, let's say, adjustments. I'm well aware that you've seen those shiny, fancy Phantom-Bombers up close, so you of all people should know warriors would need any advantage they can out there."

"That doesn't answer my goddamn question, Fallon!"

"What the hell do I look like? You are in no position to ask me anything. Whether you like it or not, you're coming with me. Now excuse me while I take your old friend out of his misery."

Agent Fallon reaches for his sword, but slightly hesitates before he dodges a large wooden spear. He demands that the assailant comes forward.

"N-no way," a shocked Keenth immediately states. "Is that really you?"

"I know, I know. I'm late to the party," Richard assures. "Sorry, boss, I was a bit caught up earlier."

"I'll have you know that an attempt on LanTech Agent's life is a crime punishable by death," Agent Fallon interrupts.

"Yeah, what of it? Besides, you survived, didn't you? More importantly, do you care to explain what a distinguished Agent such as yourself is doing out here? From what I can tell, your intentions here aren't exactly in line with those of the Invincible Empire, now are they?"

"Just like I was just telling the kid, I have no obligation to answer you. Look, things aren't exactly going how I thought they would out here. So, if you don't step aside, I'll just have to deal with you accordingly."

"Ah! Now that's something I would love to see," Richard eagerly replies. "But you'll find that taking on an opponent that, I don't know, is actually your age, might be a bit more than you can handle, Mister Agent."

"Something tells me that I'm really going to enjoy this," Agent Fallon thought to himself while releasing the waves of his Auraen. "It's been a while since I've gone all out."

"Hurry up and make your way back to the village," Richard says to Keenth as he moves Paul away from danger. "I can handle this Agent, but I can't be at two places at once."

"But Richard–"

"This isn't up for debate. You should be able to sense it now too: Kendra and the others need you, Keenth."

Keenth understood and makes his way back to Azoco Village. Agent Fallon rushes in pursuit, only to find the surrounding area covered in flames at the snap of Richard's fingers.

"It looks like you've been out here for a while. With all of this freaking rain today, I figured it wouldn't hurt to warm up a bit. Call me a nice guy, but I wouldn't want you catching a cold or anything."

"You are far too kind," Agent Fallon says as he rushes toward his opponent. "Now, allow me to show my sincere gratitude!"

Keenth focuses all of his strength toward returning to the village thinking that he's never felt Kendra's Auraen like this.

While she can be a bit rough around the edges at times, deep down Kendra's Auraen is normally genuinely warm and welcoming.

But here and now, Keenth senses something deeply raw and dark about the skirmish in Azoco.

There wasn't fighting and there definitely wasn't sparring; there was only one thing that came to Keenth's mind: Death.

"Please, please let me make it in time," Keenth thinks to himself. "Kendra, Lady Aida...Everyone...Just hold out for just a little longer."

"Is that any way to treat the Assistant Student Affairs Liaison, Keenth? I swear, this younger generation is completely out of pocket!"

"Don't you mean Assistant to the Student Affairs Liaison," Keenth quickly replies, only to realize that he's talking out loud to himself."

"Why the hell am I imagining Aamina's voice right now? Is it because Paul mentioned her before? Damn it, man...This is the last thing that I need to be worrying about right now–"

Before he can finish, the sounds of Paul's screams begin to echo through Keenth's mind. Dropping to the ground, a rapid flash of memories rush through and strike him to the very core.

"Paul...Cory...Ben...Beth…"

Keenth begins to panic uncontrollably as he remembers his friends and allies and what he believes to be their current fates.

While trying to get himself together, he wipes away what he thought to be raindrops only to see that they were tears. Then a reassuring exchange comes to mind.

"Well, don't do anything I wouldn't do..."

"Don't worry. I learned a few things that'll make you proud."

"K-Kendra...KENDRA!"

Keenth's resolve is renewed as he rushes towards his destination. Despite the injuries he sustained earlier, he is focused on helping the people he cares about.

Upon reaching Azoco, Keenth is not only shocked at how much carnage took place, but at his worst fears are realized. Finally, he manages to speak.

"That's not possible," Keenth thinks to himself as he calls out to his fallen friend. "Not you...Not you, Kendra."

As Keenth checks Kendra's pulse, she begins to cough.

"Don't use this as an excuse to use mouth-to-mouth," Kendra weakly states. "The thought...The thought of you even doing that makes me sick..."

"Yeah, yeah. Missed you too," Keenth says as he gives Kendra a reassuring smile.

"I have no idea what happened, but I've got it from here. Just hang tight, Kendra."

"T-trust me, Keenth. This isn't someone you can handle...Hell, look at me. If you still have any strength, run. Run as far away from here as possible!"

"Are you out of your mind? If they were strong enough to do all of this to the village, then–"

"Then what? She did this to our village, so it's a problem for Azoco to handle! This...this doesn't concern you, Keenth!"

"Like hell it doesn't! Sorry, but we're going to have to agree to disagree. I'm not budging on this, whether you like it or not."

"Well said, kid. Way to stand your ground. That Kendra girl is as stubborn as they come," Kusari comments. "I don't know how you people deal with her."

"We manage. The name's Keenth Hedstrom, by the way."

As Keenth begins to walk towards Kusari, he tries not to show that he's intimidated by someone who bested his mentor. On the other hand, Kusari replies to the young warrior.

"Charmed. Look, I don't know what went down outside of the village, but I'm on a job here. If you get in my way, then I'll just have to cut you up like your little friend over–"

Keenth immediately strikes Kusari only for his attack to be blocked. The fact that he was able to rush towards Kusari is something she took note of. Observing Keenth's injuries, she deduces that his movements were just above average speed.

"Keenth, huh? That was something special, wasn't it? If you had something like that under your sleeve, what took you so long to get back to the village in the first place?"

"I don't know what you're talking about."

"A bit on the slow side, are we? If you rushed here to help out the village, why didn't you just pull that trick out of your bag to get here faster?"

"Trick? Don't treat this like some type of game," Keenth shouts while raising his Auraen. "You became our problem the second you decided to step foot in Azoco!"

"Funny you say that. Your friend said something pretty similar. Tell me, how exactly do you two know one another?"

"Not that it's any of your business, but she's been training me since I got here."

"Really now? Well that makes things rather interesting, don't you think?"

"How so? What are you getting at?"

"Something tells me you didn't come back to save Azoco. Villages and cities can be rebuilt with a bit of time and effort. No, the fact that you didn't even bother asking about the others in the village tells me that you just came back for someone."

"What of it?" Keenth replies, while trying to remain focused on his opponent. "Regardless of what you think my reasons are, I'm here now. If you can understand that, then let's get this over with."

"Why are you in such a rush to end this? You must have a death wish, right?"

"Far from it. I don't know what your business is with Fallon, but I'm not going to let you people get away with any of this a second longer!"

"That's a mighty bold claim coming from a child. I'm starting to wonder if that stubbornness is your own or something you picked up from your friend over there. More importantly, whatever business I have with Fallon or anyone else is none of your concern. A job's a job, so don't make things personal."

"You do this to the village, and expect me not to take this personal?? Try saying that again after I'm done with you!!"

"Bold words," Kusari muses as she waves a storm of Auraen needles towards Keenth. "But don't get too full of yourself, boy!"

Keenth barely dodges her attack, only for Kusari to continuously repeat her assault. Keenth desperately tries to defend himself from the onslaught, but his arm is quickly penetrated by several needles.

His entire right side is now paralyzed. Keenth struggles to wield his sword with his left hand, while Kusari calmly reveals the nature of her abilities.

"Divine Willow Fang," Kusari states. "I can summon a practically endless amount of these Auraen needles. They allow me to not only penetrate most targets, but they can stop individuals from using their Auraen as well."

"H-how can an ability like that even exist?"

"To each their own. My powers do not discriminate. Man, woman, or child: if given the right price, I can use this to take down a militia with my strength alone."

"How the hell do I face something like that?" Keenth thinks to himself, before immediately considering a strategy. "Abilities aside, she's human too. There has to be a way to-"

Before Keenth can finish formulating his plan, dozens of needles strike Keenth's legs. Falling to the ground, he screams in pain, while frantically trying to move.

Knowing that the battle is reaching its end, Kusari readies one of her daggers.

"You showed promise, I'll give you that. But at the end of the day, my job is to eliminate anyone that interferes with Fallon's plan. He asked me to show restraint, but also made it very clear to kill you if necessary."

Kusari shakes her head as she raises a dagger over Keenth. In a desperate attempt to save his life, a battered Kendra intervenes, only to be stabbed in the stomach.

"Kendra? No...Why...Why would you do this?" Keenth somberly asks. "This...This wasn't supposed to happen..."

Kusari looks down as Keenth cradles his friend, feeling completely removed from everything except for Kendra's wellbeing.

With rain continuing to beat down upon the village, Keenth embraces Kendra with the hope that she would say something, anything, to reassure him that she would be okay.

Unfortunately, despite how hard he wished, he could only look on as her eyes remain closed.

Firmly gripping her blade even harder, Kusari decides to carry out her duties before being interrupted by a massive distant Efir explosion.

This brings Keenth back into the present and he is confused at Kusari preparing to depart the village.

"What are you doing?"

"Making sure Fallon doesn't get himself killed, what else does it look like?"

"Do you think you can just do this and walk away?"

"Does it really look like I gave a damn about this hellhole in the first place? What good is coming out here if my buyer gets killed in the process?"

"I don't care about that! I won't forgive you for what–"

"Would you just shut the hell up?" Kusari shouts. "It should be pretty clear that this is the best thing that could have happened to you people. This just bought you a bit longer to live, not that it matters much anyway."

"What does that even mean?"

"It means that whenever I handle this Fallon situation, you better believe that I will finish what I started with both of you."

"Why? What do you gain out of this?"

"Like I said, a job's a job. That and, if you think you can run off and hide somewhere, just know that I can trace back the Auraen of anyone that my Willow Fang has struck."

"So even if we leave the village–"

"I'll just find you wherever you go. Of course, I'll make an example out of every single person in Azoco, if that's the path you want to take. You will just come back to piles of bodies if it comes to that. I can't go around letting it seem like you got one over on me. I have a reputation to keep, after all."

"So that's what this is to you."

"No, not to me. That's just how the world works. You are nothing without what you stand for. If you are so willing to throw your life away, then feel free to follow me and die in the forest like a dog. Otherwise, enjoy the little time that you still have while you can."

With that, Kusari departs toward Fallon and Richard's battle. The sound of the rainfall was the only thing that could be heard in the village. The reality of Kusari's words hit Keenth, but before he could truly process them, his focus returned to Kendra.

"Kendra...Just give me something, anything...Please..."

The silence was more painful than any of the injuries that Keenth had sustained that day. Losing Kendra like this was something he struggled to even think about.

Holding her tightly, Keenth did not realize someone was approaching to offer support.

"Don't worry, Keenth. Somehow, she's still alive. But that will change if we don't act quickly."

"Lady Aida," Keenth exclaims. "You're okay...What about the others?"

"They're fine. When you left, Kendra and I insured that the villagers were out of harm's way. The plan was for her to meet up with you, but..."

"I'm sorry. If I were only stronger, then this...All of this, wouldn't have to happen..."

"You have nothing to apologize for, Keenth. But, again, I can't stress enough that we must move quickly to save Kendra."

"Of course. What can I do to help?"

"You? Nothing. But don't beat yourself up or anything because neither can I."

"What do you mean? You guys were able to help me after the fights on the bridge, weren't you? How is that any different to now?"

"Your case was a bit, how do I put this, different. As a matter of fact, you should know as well as I do that you surviving the way you did was a miracle. Unfortunately, we don't have the means to help Kendra when she's in such a critical condition."

"Then what happens now? We have to do something!"

"Just calm down," Lady Aida says, while revealing a small crystal necklace.

"Fortunately, I've prepared for such eventualities. Like I said, there isn't much time, so I need you to act quickly."

"And do what? What do you plan on doing? If there's nothing that can't be done here in the village, then where can Kendra get the help that she needs?"

"Isn't it obvious?" Lady Aida says as a bright light begins to emit from her crystal. "At last, it is time for you to see Sage Haden."

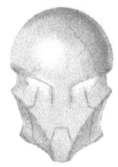

CHAPTER 10

"Sage Haden? How is that even possible?"

"What? Do you think that this crystal is glowing for my health? Now come around with Kendra and stand next to me," Lady Aida instructs. "The two of you will be at the Hatre Forest in no time."

"Gotcha," Keenth says, while lifting Kendra on his back. "What do I need to do once we get there?"

"Believe. All you have to do is believe. It seems like this Sage has been anticipating your arrival. Truth be told, I intended to send you to his forest today, but once the attack happened–"

"I understand. No need to blame yourself for anything either, Lady Aida. What's done is done. All I care about is getting help for Kendra."

"You and me both. You probably couldn't tell just by looking at us, but I've been raising Kendra since she was a little girl," Lady Aida says as the crystal's light intensifies.

"She's the closest thing to a daughter that I've ever had. It pains me to place such a heavy burden on you like this, but please save her.

Without Kendra, this village's days are numbered. Without Kendra, my heart cannot…"

"There's nothing for you to worry about. I'll make sure that she's taken care of. You have my word," Keenth swears with his words comforting not just Aida, but himself.

"Thank you. The release is now complete. Once I place my hand on your shoulder, you will arrive at your destination within a few moments. It may not be much, but this is the best way I can help you on your journey. I leave the rest to you, Keenth."

The young warrior nodded as the village elder raised her necklace, engulfing Keenth and Kendra with a brimming, sublime light.

Leaving the fate of Kendra and the village in Keenth's hands, Lady Aida broke down in tears as she stood alone in the middle of Azoco.

"It saddens me to put you through all of this. Perhaps if we had made wiser decisions along the way, we wouldn't be forced to ask so much of you," Lady Aida thought to herself as the rain began to subside.

"But the time for regret and reflection is gone. The future is in your young hands now and I have faith you will make things right moving forward."

As Lady Aida continued her silent prayers, Keenth and Kendra safely made their arrival. Unlike the lush forests of Azoco and the rest of Tortuga, it seemed as though they were in a thick jungle than anything else.

While the rain had calmed down, dark clouds and a foreboding fog surrounded the two young travelers.

After what felt like hours, Keenth realized that night had fallen and there was still no Sage in sight. He almost began to voice his frustrations, but Keenth remembered Lady Aida's guidance to believe.

"Don't worry, Kendra, we'll be there before you know it. Though if you were awake, you would've called me out for walking in circles."

"After all of this time, you would think that you would learn your way around a forest."

"This voice...That cloak, those robes...Is it really–"

"It's been a while, Keenth. As much as I would love to catch up with you right now, we need to get her to safety right away," Cory replies. "If you follow me, we'll be arriving at the temple shortly."

The moonlight guides Keenth and Cory deeper through the forest until at long last, they finally make it to the forest temple. More properly known as the Hatre Temple, it is a secluded location that isn't easily accessible to most.

The atmosphere is as haunting as it is serene, and Cory gives Keenth an assuring smile to let him know that things would work for the best.

She removes her cloak, and asks Keenth to lay Kendra on a wooden altar towards the center of the temple before positioning herself to quietly meditate.

Keenth attempts to ask Cory what she is doing, but he is interrupted by the presence of an unfamiliar Auraen behind him. He quickly turns, but no one is there.

When Keenth refocuses on Kendra, but he sees a mysterious individual synchronized in meditation with Cory.

"Are you are...?"

"Just a moment," the individual replies with their hand over Kendra's forehead. "We have time to get to formalities soon, but right now my focus on Ms. Leight over here."

"How do you know her name?"

"I wouldn't be much of a Sage if I didn't know who you two were, don't you agree? Fortunately, she has tremendous willpower. It'll take some work, but I believe Kendra will be okay."

Despite this being the first time meeting him, Keenth feels a tremendous amount of reassurance at this revolution.

A true to word gentle giant, the Sage's large intricate robes are a lavish green compared to what Cory normally wears.

His long dark hair, matching beard, and stern brown eyes left little doubt to Keenth who he was face-to-face with.

"...You must be Lord Haden?"

"That is correct. It is a pleasure to finally meet you, Keenth. You have gone through many hardships, haven't you?"

"To be honest, I don't even know where to start..."

"That's fine. I'm well aware of what happened at the Academy, on the bridge, and recently, over in Azoco. That is quite a bit for someone your age to go through."

"Wait, how do you know all of that? I could understand you knowing most through Cory, but Kendra and I were the only ones fighting in Azoco and not too long ago."

"As strange as it may sound to you, the world spoke to me. It only tells the truth to those who are willing to listen."

"The world? Sorry, but with all due respect, I–"

"I know, I know. It sounds like ramblings of a crazy old hermit, but that is the truth. As you've surely seen through Cory, users of Hatre are in touch with Earth-based abilities. But these abilities are often mistaken only as the means to manipulate the world around us."

"What do you mean? Like you said, I saw Cory using Hatre quite a bit when we fought alongside one another."

"The common misunderstanding is that the elements are here to be used by us, when the truth is that these elements are here to be used alongside us. If you spent time in Azoco, then surely you know that everything is made of Auraen. The world we live in serves as the backdrop to all events–past, present, and future."

"So, when you say the world spoke to you…"

"I normally interpret the messages through my dreams and share what I know accordingly. I believe you've had similar experiences as well, haven't you, Keenth?"

"Yes. I didn't think anyone would believe me if I told them, but I had vivid dreams about the attack on Agent Keyes more times than I care to count."

"But that isn't all, is it?"

"No, it isn't. The strange thing is, I started having the dreams before Agent Keyes and the others were attacked. It was almost as if–"

"I see. Do you remember any other specific dreams, Keenth?"

"No, nothing like that. The only other dreams that come to mind were mostly memories of my time growing up in Colonia."

"Are you okay with sharing those, Keenth?"

"They don't matter right now. Sorry, but what exactly do we gain from talking about dreams? Listen, Kusari and Fallon are probably on their way back to Azoco, so please tell me how you plan on saving the village."

"How do I do what now? Apologizes, but you must be mistaken. I have no intention of saving Azoco."

"What the hell did you just say? You saw what they did to Kendra and I, so why aren't you doing anything to help us?"

"Do you hear yourself right now, Keenth? Asking how I plan on saving Azoco? Asking why I am not doing anything to help? Where is your shame? Where is your pride as a warrior?"

"Pride? Do you think this has anything to do with pride? I've seen

Cory's abilities and, if she's just your apprentice, then you should be more than enough to—"

"Handle your problems? You should be thankful Kendra isn't conscious to hear this because—"

"Don't you dare speak her name," Keenth shouts, causing the foundations of the temple to shake. Realizing this, Keenth begins to apologize to Haden before being admonished.

"Sorry? Yes, you should be. Especially considering that you have everything you need to define your own fate."

"I don't think you understand. I barely made it out of Azoco alive and I'm honestly in no position to fight them off again any time soon."

"While I do agree that time is not a luxury at the moment, it seems as though I need to explain this in a way that you would understand. Cory, please continue on here until I get back."

"Get back? Kendra needs your help, so what could be more important than that?"

"Saving your world, Keenth. Now, quiet down. I'll be able to answer your questions in a place that you should be very familiar with."

"Wait, somewhere that I'm familiar with—"

Keenth is cut off by an abrupt boom that removed them from the Hatre Temple. Once he opens his eyes, he is surprised to see that the Sage was true to his word.

There was no doubt that in his mind that he was now hearing the nostalgic sounds of waves reaching the shores of his childhood.

"This can't be...Are we in…"

"Yes, Keenth. We're here in Colonia. I take it has been some time since you've been home, hasn't it?"

"I didn't think something like this was even possible. It's nothing at all like how Cory and Lady Aida did things."

"I guess me being, I don't know, a Sage might have something to do with it. But what do I know?" Haden points out toward the ocean. "This looks like quite the place to call home, Keenth."

"It really is, but what exactly are we doing here?"

"Right. So, something told me you weren't willing to open up about a few things in the Temple. I believe that you would feel more comfortable to do so here. Is that something that you agree with?"

"Yeah, I guess," Keenth replies as he looks around, lost in thought. "I'm sorry, what was the question again?"

"The question was about dreams. Namely, the memories of growing up here."

"Oh, yes...It has been a while since I have had them, so they're a bit hazy. What I remember most are voices and the sounds of things going around near the beaches."

"You've gotta work with me a bit here, Island Boy."

"Right, right...So there's a younger voice that I definitely recognize as my own. The other belongs to Mark, my older brother. I can't put my finger on it, but it sounds like we're racing one another or something."

"Racing on the beach, huh? You must have been full of energy. Just the thought of it makes my knee begin to hurt, Keenth."

"Really? That sounds like something an old timer like Renzel would say. Speaking of which, just how old are you anyway?"

"Hey now, let's just focus on those dreams before you get distracted again."

"Alright, fine. So, we run on and on as if the world was our playground. As tiring as it may sound, I wouldn't trade moments like those for the world."

"I believe that. Still, don't you think it is a little dangerous to be so young and running around the beach alone like that? Was this Renzel person around? If so, what was he thinking?"

"Renzel? He's been our village elder for as long as I can remember. He wouldn't feel right letting us play around alone like that. It's fine since we were definitely in good hands at the time."

"Really now? So, who was there then?"

"My dad," Keenth replies, feeling bittersweet emotions. "Funny that you ask because it's been a while since I could remember his face so clearly. Mark and I were always told how much we look like him."

"I see. So, what are you all doing around the beach in this dream?"

"Well, Mark and I are racing off to meet up with my dad. He would normally watch us from cliffs, like the ones that we are standing on right now. Only this time, he had a surprise waiting for us when we reached him."

"A surprise, huh? I bet you were really excited. Is it something that you still keep around these days?"

"Why don't you take a look for yourself?" Keenth replies as he hands Haden his sword. "Even though we were young, my dad gave us matching swords. He figured that since we were his boys, we would be more than capable of handling them properly."

"That's really something," Haden states as he returns the heirloom. "Do you know if there's any particular reason why he gave you this that day?"

"I honestly couldn't tell you. My dad would just have these feelings, you know? He'd follow his gut on a lot of things and taught us to trust the process."

"That's respectable. Is there anything else that you remember from the dream?"

"I wish I did, but that's pretty much where it ends. The swords that he gave us were smaller versions of the one that he used for years. Just when he would start to explain why he gave them to us, I normally begin to wake up."

"Very interesting...Thanks for sharing, Keenth. Now, why do you think those memories return through your dreams?"

"I don't know, maybe because island life these days can be pretty boring?"

"Keenth..."

"Okay, okay. It's just not something that I go out of my way to think about often. Do you think that's weird?"

"No, not at all. If anything, it helps telling you what I'm about to say slightly easier."

"Really? What's that?"

"Keenth, I think it would be for the best if you stay here and never return to Tortuga."

"Is this some sort of joke? Why the hell would you say even that?"

"You should understand that this isn't something that I would say lightly. There is clearly something about the past that is calling to you. Until you come to terms with that, you will never be at peace with your future."

"So that's it, huh? Cory and the others risked their lives for me to meet you only to hear this? Thanks for absolutely nothing! Now get out of my way, I have to make my way back to the Azoco."

"What do you hope to accomplish there, Keenth?"

"The only time airships are here is when they make their way out from the mainland. If I could get a boat from Renzel and the others, then I...Wait, what's it to you anyway?"

"If your goal is to return to Tortuga, then why aren't you asking to be brought there the same way you came here?"

"Because you are worthless to me," Keenth shouts. "You've done nothing, but waste my time and shattered the last ounces of hope that I had left. Are you happy? Is that what you want to hear?"

"If that's how you feel, then so be it. I can't force you to do anything, Keenth. If I leave now, then there's still time for Kendra to–"

"Kendra? What do you plan on doing with her?"

"To do what Aida originally sent you to me for, or did you forget already? While I will be able to help her recover, it's unlikely that her strength will be at a level where she can defeat your opponents from earlier."

"Wait, no! If you do that then–"

"Yes, she'll more than likely die when they decide to return to Azoco Village."

"And that's okay to you? Do you even hear yourself right now?"

"Not to speak on Kendra's behalf, but I'm sure she'd accept this. She is the guardian of her village. Her purpose is to protect Azoco with her life and she wouldn't think twice about sacrificing herself for the sake of her people. Tell me that I'm wrong, Keenth."

"No, you're right. You're absolutely right. But that still doesn't make it okay. What good am I if I'm not around to join the battle as well? After all, I'm part of the reason why Azoco was attacked in the first place."

"You would only get in their way, Keenth. You've made it as far as you have thanks to being guided by Kendra and the others, but these opponents are of a completely different caliber. I've spoken enough on this. If you really want to do something for Kendra, have faith in her and believe that–"

"He wasn't here to protect us!"

"Keenth…"

"When my dad died, Mark and I were all we had for one another. As time went on, we realized how cold this world can really be. For years, we learned how to defend ourselves on our own..."

The Sage quietly listened as the raw anger continued to flow through Keenth's words. Whether he knew it or not, this was the most liberated that his soul has been in years. Between the events of the past and the ones from the Training Academy until now, Keenth's emotions had finally reached their boiling point.

"But just when we finally got to a place where we could proudly stand on our own two feet, Mark up and died on me too."

"I'm sorry, I didn't know that. But Keenth–"

"So, you know what, Haden, you're right, I'm mad. I'm pissed. I've got a whole lot of things to work through, but the last thing I'll have on my conscience is losing Kendra because I wasn't strong enough to do anything!!"

"Keenth! Keenth!!"

Haden's words caused Keenth to realize that the waves behind him were violently crashing then due to his emotions getting the best of him.

Staggered at the thought of his Auraen having such an effect on his surroundings, he began to calm down as the Sage wandered toward him.

"I hope this will help explain what I was trying to tell you earlier, Keenth. Clearly there's something very special about you," Haden continues as he uses his own Auraen to calm the waters.

"Cory and the others would not put themselves out there the way that they did if that was not the case. Like I said before, the world speaks to me. It is my duty as a Sage is to tell the truth to those who are willing to listen."

"But what does that have to do with everything that has been going on lately?"

"You've been asleep for years, Keenth. I believe that your abilities, your true abilities, have been sealed away by your deep-rooted feelings of anger, among other things. They have only recently begun to rise above the surface because there is a part of you that knows...Knows that it is time for your awakening, Keenth."

"My awakening? What does that mean?"

"I'm sure you've wondered why the abilities of Kendra and the others are drastically different from yours. The reason for this is because they're at a point where they can harness their true power. You, on the other hand, are still shackled down by your own fears and insecurities. You're suppressing what you are really capable of."

"Then please...Please show me how to awaken. I'll do whatever it takes to make things right."

"Normally, I would agree, but here is where we hit a fork in the road. Understand that by doing this, nothing will be the same. Changing fate is not something that should be taken lightly. This is why I am only offering you to choose between two directions as there is no going back."

"On one hand, I can open the path to knowledge beyond your wildest dreams. Knowledge that would reveal the answers to all of the questions regarding your past. Everything about your family and their purpose in the world. Surely, that would put the pains of your soul to rest."

"I can remove the shackles preventing you from truly living your fullest potential. With this, you may have the capabilities to avenge what has recently been taking place in Tortuga."

Keenth stood in silence under the moonlit sky, pondering.

"You don't have to say anything, Keenth. Words simply are not necessary when the conviction in your eyes says it all. You've already made your decision, so now it is just a matter of getting you there."

"Sorry, but getting me where?"

"Come, Keenth. It's time to leave your dreams in the past and save Azoco."

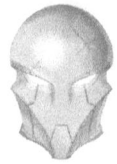

CHAPTER 11

October 3rd – 2:20 PM

"Hey, hey! J-just wait right there! Give me a chance to explain," Claude pleads to an unforgiving Weiss. "Trust me when I say that it's not what it looks like!"

"Shut your damn mouth! We caught you red-handed, tinkering around in our caverns, so what else is it supposed to look like! It's been just over a day since you heathens ran through Azoco and you just couldn't help yourself, could you?"

"No, you don't understand! If I don't disable the signal from the Bomber, then—"

Before he could finish, Claude is struck by several Auraen needles.

Knowing all too well who they came from, Weiss and the others look ahead to see Kusari approaching the village.

"You really need to learn to quit while you're ahead," Kusari states. "But the fact that you found the machine means you aren't completely useless."

"Kusari, you monster…"

"Don't give me that. Things didn't go exactly as planned, but you've done your part. Now give me Fallon's coordinates so we can get out of this trash pile."

"W-wait, you don't know where Jimmy is?"

"If I did, do you think I would bother asking you? If you understand that, then give me the coordinates. I won't ask you again."

"No. You won't be getting them from me, Kusari."

"…I'm sorry, what was that?"

"You heard me. You ain't getting a word out of me! The only thing holding you back from wasting me or the rest of the village is knowing where Jimmy is. I don't know what he put in your head, but you went overboard here in Azoco. It'll be a cold day in hell before I—"

Having lost her patience, Kusari swiftly retracts the blades protruding from Claude. As the man begins to bleed out, Kusari makes her intentions clear to him and the rest of the villagers in the area.

"Azoco has been a thorn on my side ever since the second I set foot here. Factor that in this worthless excuse for a human dragging his feet over an otherwise simple task and that means you people are going to see my bad side."

"Not that I can't find Fallon on my own, but it's the principle of the thing," Kusari continues, as she arms herself with a dagger. "Watch carefully as I drag him out of his misery as I'll be doing the same for each and every one of you."

Kusari launches her weapon at Claude, only for it to stop just short of his throat. To his surprise, the dagger was caught by a seemingly unfamiliar young man.

Donning a large brown cloak over a black sleeveless shirt, this warrior calmly faces Kusari as Claude ponders who he might be.

"W-What name do you go by, blondie?"

"So, the prodigal son returns," Kusari states. "I'm surprised you actually showed your face here, Keenth!"

"Should you really be all that surprised?" Keenth replies, continuing to stare Kusari down. "If memory serves me correctly, we didn't finish our session from the other day."

"Ah, a second chance at life and you're willing to throw it away so easily. Very well, I'll show you what I'm really capable of. Don't think for a second that I'm going to take this fight out of the village because they're all next."

"That's fine. After all, I want them to see this."

"Really now? Well, keep that same energy when I leave you bleeding out and full of holes just like—"

In a flash, Kusari barely dodges the dagger that Keenth throws in her direction. Examining the gash on her forehead, she quickly realizes her opponent was not to be trifled with.

"You are not allowed to speak her name," Keenth firmly states. "Azoco's guardian isn't here, so I will be defending the village in their place."

"As if I would think twice about taking orders from someone like you! Don't get arrogant, boy!"

Kusari rushes forward and punches Keenth directly across the jaw, only for him to unflinchingly stare back at her.

Astonished, she attempts to do this again, only for Keenth to catch her fist and counter with a strike to her chest.

"Kusari, was it? Let me know whenever you're ready to take this seriously."

"What the hell is going on here?" Kusari thinks. "Is this really the same kid I fought? How much can change in such a short amount of time?"

"Divine Willow Fang," Keenth states. "That's your special ability, isn't it?"

"Yeah, that's my attack. What of it?"

"I want you to use it, Kusari. All of it. Right here, right now."

"What? You really must really want to die, don't you?"

"No, I won't die. You seem to question what's going on in this fight right now, so I want you to use your best attack on me, so that there's no room for any doubts," Keenth explains. "Now go on and get this over with. I don't have all day."

"Who the hell...?" Kusari begins to ask as she readies her attack. "Just who the hell do you think you're talking to??"

Kusari unleashes hundreds of Auraen needles at point-blank range, causing massive clouds of dirt to arise across Azoco. She continues her barrage for several minutes until her stamina finally begins to waver.

As the wind blows through the village, Kusari is dumbfounded at seeing only Keenth's tattered cloak on the ground where he once stood.

"It's impossible," Kusari states. "There isn't even a drop of blood in sight. Did he...Did he just vanish?"

"You know if you could sense me, then you wouldn't have to ask that question."

Kusari attempts to turn around, but Keenth releases a pulse of Auraen with enough force to send her crashing toward the village outskirts.

Kusari shouts in rage at not only being bested by her opponent, but the truth in his words.

"I don't care what you think this is. But you're far from my level, Keenth! Don't you dare say otherwise!"

"You know, believe it or not, I agree with you. After all, if we were on the same level, then you would've sensed me just now and when I made my way back to Azoco village, wouldn't you? I'm sure a warrior like yourself understands what this means, don't you?"

"Shut up!!"

Kusari launches a handful of Auraen needles, only for Keenth to catch and discard them with ease.

For the first time in many years of fighting, Kusari feels the walls closing in. As she curses herself at allowing the battle to end in her opponent's favor, Keenth redirects her focus.

"Whether you believe it or not, you should know that I'm not your enemy," Keenth begins. "Kendra was right...This was a fight between you and Azoco. I'm just standing in her place for the time being. Just tell me where Fallon is and this can end right now."

"No, no! That's where you're wrong," Kusari shouts. "The fight never ends for people like me! If you call yourself a warrior, then you should understand that too!"

"So, it really comes down to this," Keenth thinks as he draws his blade. "Like Sage Haden said, nothing would be the same after this."

"So, you finally decided to use your sword," Kusari states as Auraen needles silently surround their battleground. "That means I can show you finally cut you down accordingly..."

"I see. I'm ready whenever you are."

"There's something that you need to understand, Keenth. You should know that my ability is unlike most others. I focus all of my strength to create needles that run through any and all opponents my way...But what do you think happens if the needles are focused in another way?"

"Kusari, what do you...?"

More needles rapidly surround them and, to Keenth's shock, the forest is encased with thousands of them. Wondering if they will rain down on him, Kusari clarifies her signature ability.

"The Wrath of the Divine Willow Fang is truly seen when I harness all of my Auraen towards complete and utter destruction," Kusari states as the needles forcefully return to her. "Prepare yourself, Keenth. You are not walking away alive from this."

Keenth slightly winces at the sight of needles protruding from Kusari's body, sensing an unbelievable increase in her Auraen.

But, understanding that there truly is no backing down from this now, Keenth raised his Auraen to a level that stuns Kusari.

"Tell me, Keenth. What the hell do get your power to such a strong level?"

"I let go. I finally decided to let go of what I couldn't control and chose to fight for what matters the most to me."

"Yeah, and what's that?"

"If we survive this, then I'll tell you after I find Fallon."

"I see. Well, fair enough," Kusari says as she readies the second and final dagger to her disposal. With a split moment to do so, she remembers the battered, yet determined Keenth from their last bout.

"This is it...Prepare yourself," Kusari muses at the thought of them being worlds apart before, yet finally realizing that Keenth has now truly found himself.

The sounds of their respective Auraens roaring over one another render everything else inaudible as the two rushed forward for the final clash. A trail of deep, dark red blood is seen on the ground as Auraen needles slowly begin to fade.

"You focused so much power in increasing your strength that you compromised your defenses," Keenth thinks to himself as Kusari lies quietly in defeat. "Had that fearsome attack of yours reached me, then I..."

Suddenly, there is the sound of an airship landing nearby. The make and model make it clear that it belongs to a LanTech Agent, so he readies himself accordingly. To his surprise, it was not Agent Fallon who stepped forward. Before Keenth could ask, a spirited man introduces himself.

"Ah, I hope I'm not intruding or anything, but you wouldn't happen to have ran into an Agent around these parts, have you?"

"I'm sorry, and you are...?"

"Ah, right, Giles. Agent Roland Giles. You're that Keenth kid, right?

"Well, yes. I mean, how do you know my name?"

"Not to brag or anything, but I helped Weiss in bringing you to Azoco village in the first place! Though I have to admit, you look pretty different compared to over a week ago. Did you get a haircut or something? That and I take it you weren't holding back with eating your veggies."

"Ah, that's right! I know Mr. Weiss helped to save me, but he didn't say anything about an Agent!"

"Well, to his defense, he didn't know that I was...well, am, an Agent at the time. I was doing some investigation work on Prospear and ran into him. Don't worry, I broke things down to everyone in the village not too long afterwards."

"Sure, I guess. But what's this about an Agent?"

"Right, so I'm looking for an Agent Fallon. James Fallon. We are doing an—"

"Fallon! Yeah, I know him alright! He...we ran into each other not too long ago."

"I figured as much. The signal off of his airship ran cold around here recently. We give each other free reign as far as investigations go, but this is hardly the time to lose track of one of our own."

"I understand and I wish I could help. But I'm sorry to tell you that..."

"Hey listen, bud, and listen carefully. I can see it in your face: try not to carry the weight of the world on your shoulders. I know that's easier said than done with everything that's been going on lately, but it's something worth considering."

"Thanks, Sir. I appreciate it."

"Anytime! While I'm here, do you mind telling me what happened just now? I landed after everything settled because it looked like a warzone from a distance. I see the defeated warrior over there, but where did the rest of fighters head off to?".

"I...um...How do I explain? There wasn't a group of fighters or anything. It was just me."

"So, I reach out to you, and you think it's okay to lie to my face. Is that the type of program we're on, Kenneth with an extra vowel? Is that where we stand?"

"No, I'm serious! It started in the village, but I brought the fight out here to avoid any more damage."

"Wow...You aren't kidding, are you? There's something about some of the abilities I sense here that are oddly familiar?"

"What do you mean, Sir?"

"Giles is fine. But what I mean is that it reminds me of Silverdale, an Ira ability to manipulate wind to increase your speed and agility. I would know because I use it quite a bit myself!"

"Really? I've never met someone with that type of power before!"

"Cool, right? Well, yes and no. You see, it feels similar to Silverdale, but there's something off. Something different...Keenth, what exactly happened since I brought you to the village?"

"Well, Sir. I mean, Giles, I—"

Agent Giles shushes Keenth as he hears someone making their way to his airship.

He quietly picks up a stone and lightly uses Ira to stop the would-be vandal in their tracks. Screaming in pain, this individual threatens legal action.

"Really, Claude? You are telling me to lawyer up when you try to break into my vehicle?"

"It's a free region," Claude replies. "I'll never forgive you even if you beg me to!"

"You know this guy," Keenth quietly asks. "More importantly, don't move Claude! You tried to steal my cloak!"

"Unfortunately, I do. His father is a pretty decent person. Our friend, Claude, here and his brother on the other hand…"

"Is ready to get the heck out of this village! It's been nothing but a nightmare for me! Ro, listen, trust me when I say that you don't want anything to do with Azoco!"

"You sure? Because they were pretty friendly to me and they practically never deal with Agents around these parts."

"You got lucky! Anyway, I gotta come clean with you when it comes to your boy, Jimmy."

"Jimmy? Oh, you mean Fallon. What about him? Have you seen him lately?"

"Seen him? He's the reason why I'm down here in the first place. I can explain to you on the way back, but—"

"No, Claude. You can go ahead and show him what you saw in the cavern," Keenth says. "Intentional or not, you held your ground a bit when it came to defending Azoco from Kusari, so we owe you that much."

"Really? Thanks, Keeny! Glad we're on speaking terms! Hell, I know I've done my fair share reading about you up until now?"

"Reading? Do you care to elaborate on that to make it sound any less disturbing?"

"Jimmy had quite the file on you, my boy. A ton of Academy stuff, like your entry date, test scores, ability projections...all of that. Combine that with his obsession with tracking down that Bomber model and—"

"Wait, Bomber model? As in those Phantom-Bombers? What does Fallon have to do with those?" Agent Giles asks.

"Oh, so you guys really didn't know...I see," Claude replies. "Well, now's probably the best time to get you all up to speed on things. About Jimmy and the Bombers. Most importantly, Keeny, where his hideout is."

"...Trust me when I say it's a place you know very well."

*

October 3rd – 2:45PM

The winds calmly blow through the forest where Keenth and Agent Giles carefully listen to Claude share his knowledge regarding the Phantom-Bombers. These machines were unlike anything Claude had encountered before.

Their sentience and flawless adaptability to battle in real-time made them exceptionally dangerous. You never knew when or where they would strike next.

"Is there any way of knowing how many are out there?" Agent Giles asks.

"I honestly couldn't tell you. My guess is maybe hundreds or thousands. Jimmy kept a lot of details to himself."

"Seeing how he made finding the one out in Azoco a priority, I think you may be able to figure out an exact number once you reverse engineer that thing."

"Ah, I couldn't say it better myself. Get that machine over to my airship, Claude. We will be leaving for Sadeena shortly."

"W-wait, huh? I'm doing what now??"

"Isn't it obvious? While I was able to stop Kusari's bleeding, she'll definitely need medical attention. That and you clearly have a better grasp on these machines than most. It makes the most sense."

"I know, I know...But of all places, why Sadeena? Tortuga is one thing, but Sadeena is pretty much the LanTech metropolis! How do I know that I'll even make it out of there alive?"

"Because you'll be alongside Agent Giles and he's an honorable man from what I can tell," Keenth answers. "If he says heading there is for the best, then there shouldn't be any reason not to believe him."

"Thanks for the praise, but how exactly did you come to that conclusion?"

"When it comes to sensing Auraen, it isn't just a simple matter of being able to tell how powerful someone is. In a way, you can also grasp their intentions as well. I'm not getting the feeling that you are someone that should not be trusted."

"I see, I see. Well, thanks for the vote of confidence, Keenth. So how about you? What do you plan on doing from here?"

"G-Good question," Keenth replies, at a loss for words. "I was kind of expecting Fallon to be here. But since he isn't, I guess I'll just head out to his hideout up north. The thing is that, if I do, then the village—"

"What about it?" a voice replies as they approach Keenth. "You're too young to be stressing about every little thing, you know."

"Lady Aida!"

"Ah, Keenth! I am truly glad to see that the strength in your eyes says that your encounter with Sage Haden went exceptionally well."

"Yeah, better than I could imagine! But we can catch up on all of that later. Let's head back to the village in case Fallon decides to attack Azoco again."

"You're a stubborn one, aren't you? You were already provided a path towards Fallon, so what is this nonsense about you staying down here?"

"There isn't much to think about. I owe Azoco an enormous debt for everything its villagers have done for me. You all have literally saved my life more than once. Who am I to just walk away now?"

"Human. You'd be human, just like the rest of us. Listen Keenth, you can't tether your life to the fate of our village like this. As you clearly know, there are bigger things out there right now. Your strength is needed to protect Tortuga, no, Hasania as a whole. Don't let fear hold you back on this one."

"I know, I know. But what happens if Azoco is—"

"Believe. I told you that for a reason. Our village will be fine, you have my word. You cannot put such a heavy burden on your shoulders, especially when we are all here to support one another. Have faith, Keenth."

Keenth nodded at Lady Aida, before sprinting northbound. When he was finally at a safe distance from the others, he leaped over the surrounding trees and used his Auraen to dash through the sky.

"He's definitely an interesting one. Anyway, I'll be heading out now. Sorry to say this, but I can't be at two places at once, Ma'am. If it's alright with you, I can deploy a small team out here to protect the village," Agent Giles offered.

"Thanks for the offer, dear. But there's help on their way to defend Azoco."

"Do you honestly think they are enough to fend off the Phantom-Bombers?"

"Knowing them, they can handle it. After all, it wouldn't be their first time."

*

October 3rd – 8:25 PM

In the hours since Keenth had departed Azoco village, the sun quietly set on Tortuga. A warm orange sky covers the remnants of the Prospear Bridge where a LanTech airship lands.

An Agent makes their way towards an individual hidden in the shadows. After letting out a sigh of disappointment, he expresses his thoughts.

"Of all of the places to meet, why would you choose here? Is there anything else here worth investigating, Agent Fallon?"

"Really, man? What's with the 'Agent Fallon' stuff, even when no one is even around? Let's keep it on a first name basis for my sanity, David. Is that alright with you?" James responds. "After all, I'm not exactly here in official business."

"Fine, James. We'll do it your way. Just answer my question about why we are meeting here."

"It's been a couple of weeks since the attack on this bridge, yet it could pass for a ghost town. It's a real shame how bad these attacks have shaken people up around here."

"That is to be expected. People tend to put their safety first, even at the risk of staying away from landmarks as iconic as Prospear or the Training Academy. But given time, they'll return as if nothing happened."

"Really? How do you figure, David?"

"It's human nature, really. People only care for what you have done or what you've done for them lately. Once we get a few reconstruction teams out here, they'll come flooding back in no time."

"Yeah, I guess you're right. Hopefully this happens sooner rather than later."

"Oh? Why the rush? Don't tell me that this place holds sentimental value to you all of a sudden?"

"Ha! Well, maybe, though it wouldn't be all of a sudden. The center of the bridge is where I was commissioned as an Agent about five years ago."

"Ah, that's right. Has it been that long already?"

"Well, you'd remember if you showed up..."

"James, we've talked about this. I was doing an investigation near the Cordela border and—"

"Yeah, yeah. The mission always takes priority. I get that, trust me. It's just that, I don't know, it would be nice if you would consider how much of a milestone that was for me."

"Right. You're absolutely right. My apologies for that, James. If it means anything to you, I'll keep that in mind when you're promoted to an Elite Agent one day."

"Me? An Elite? Get out of here! Sure, you have a pretty good shot, but I barely made the cut as an Agent as is. Thanks for the thought, though."

"Ha, the only thing that would hold you back is yourself. If being an Elite or dare I say even a future Executive Officer is a goal, then fully dedicate yourself to that."

"Interesting. I never thought I would hear that from you. Who knows, I might be the next Commanding Officer at that rate.

Commander Fallon! It has a pretty good ring to it, doesn't it?"

"It all depends on which Fallon you're referring to," David jokes.

For the first time in many years, the Fallon Brothers shared a genuine laugh with one another.

While time and certain events slowly pushed them apart over time, the siblings finally had a sense of relief, despite recent events.

Still, as their black overcoats signified, they were both first and foremost Agents of the LanTech Empire.

In the wake of a series of attacks in Tortuga, it was their obligation to hold those behind these events accountable.

"So, James, are you going to tell me what happened to your arm?" the elder Fallon asks. "It seems like you've run into some trouble lately."

"Oh, this? Well, when you are diving into an investigation like this, a few fights here and there come with the territory," James replies, gazing down at the bottom half of his right sleeve which was burned off.

"Where did this happen? There's still time to dispatch infantry to track down whoever—"

"Hey, it's nothing to worry about. I already handled it. But, look, I know you're a pretty busy guy and you don't have a lot of time to waste. There's something important that we need to talk about."

"Sure, what's on your mind, James?"

"More than you could imagine. But what I brought you here for was to talk about the Phantom-Bombers."

"What about them? There have only been fragments of clues left behind during both of their attacks. Truth be told, I was hoping that you would be able to unveil more while—"

"Cut the act, David. You know exactly what I'm getting at. How advanced they are, their destructive potential. There's only one person who would be able to design machines on this level. A person that we're all too familiar with."

"Agent Keyes," David soberly replies. "Sure, the idea has crossed my mind, but it makes absolutely no sense for him to have a hand in any of this."

"I know, but hear me out. He doesn't seem like the type to do something like this, but that doesn't mean he wasn't forced to by the Executive Counsel or something. How else would you explain this, David?"

"Honestly, I can't. But for you to even suggest something like this would be grounds for major discipline. Please tell me you have something to back this up."

"That's where you come in. Agents Connors, Giles, and yourself were directly mentored by Keyes. It's safe to say that the three of you would know more about him than the rest of us. Is there something— anything—that could help us make any sense of this?"

"Before we go any further, why are you asking me? Haven't you been working alongside Agents Connors and Giles during this investigation? Why haven't you approached them with this?"

"It's because I trust you, David. If this is as big as we think it is, what's to say they wouldn't think twice to take me out to cover their tracks? We've gotta do something before the next attack!"

"Next attack? Just how much do you know about these machines?"

"David, you've gotta trust me on this one. There's so much to get into, but we can't do it here. I have an airship docked on the other side of the bridge. It's not a LanTech issued one, so we'd be off the grid for the time being. If we leave now, then we—"

"Wait, what are you suggesting? You do realize how insane this is, don't you? It is one thing to suggest treason among the ranks, but how do you think it would look moving forward without going through the proper channels?"

"How would it look? Get over yourself, David! If what I'm saying is right, then some of our own took it upon themselves to eliminate a part of the proper channels you are so obsessed about! We have to do something about it and we don't have time to debate this. So, tell me, are you in or are you out?"

"...I'm in. This is absolutely insane, but I'm in. If it's something that you are so passionate about, then I'll support you on this one. You'd better hope, for both of our sakes, that you are right about this, James."

"Is that any way to talk to a future Elite Agent?" James replies, attempting to add some levity to the situation. "We'll talk more on the way over there, sounds good?"

James looked over at his brother who stood in complete silence. Wondering what could have caused such a sudden change in his demeanor. Before he could ask what was going on, David ominously stated that he had to go.

"You're leaving? What could be more important than this?"

"It was an urgent message from Forensics. I need to leave right away."

"Forensics? Tell your people that it could wait. Needless to say, but what we have going on is way more important than whatever they're stuck on."

"That's the thing, James. This message didn't come from any of my subordinates–it came from Agent Keyes."

"What?? How the hell is that even possible?"

"It isn't...It can't be possible...As the Forensics Lead, I conducted Agent Keyes' autopsy myself. There's just no way that he is alive."

"Then maybe someone is using his device to contact you?"

"I doubt it. Unlike the rest of us, Agents at the Elite Level use communicators that are bio-authenticated. In other words, Agent Keyes' device has been inoperable since he's been dead–that is, for over a month."

"This just doesn't add up. Maybe one of the Agents is doing this just to mess with you? Come on, David, let's head over to find out right now!"

"Sorry, James, but I'm heading there alone. The fact that this message was sent to me must be for a reason. The last thing that I would want to do is involve you with this."

"Involve me? I'm the lead on the Keyes Investigation, so what makes you think that—"

"James! You asked me to trust you and I'm asking you to do the same. If it means anything to you, I'm just going there to see if it's something the rebels set up. If you don't hear back from me within the hour, feel free to come down with full force."

"Fine, you win. Just be careful, David. I'll be there if you need me, okay?"

"That's Agent Fallon, and of course. I know you've got my back, brother."

Agent David Fallon bids farewell and departs as his brother looks on. As his airship flies off into the distance, Agent James Fallon calls over to an unknown individual.

"You can come out now," Agent Fallon instructs. "It seems as though having you there as backup was unnecessary after all."

"If I may, Sir, there is nothing wrong with taking extra precautions," Paul answers as he approaches. "If yesterday told us anything, it is that you can never be too safe these days."

"I guess you're right. That and you gave me a bit of a scare there the other day. I'm glad to see that you're back on track."

"Of course, Sir. Speaking of which, will we be departing for Azoco to eliminate Hedstrom and the others?"

"Azoco? No, that's old news. If Kusari or Claude haven't gotten back to me by now, then there's no point in heading back there. We hardly have that kind of time to waste."

"I understand. Then what will happen if someone traces back the machine in their village to you? Wouldn't all of this be for nothing?"

"You really must have hit your head hard. After tonight, there won't be an Azoco village to worry about. But there's no point in chatting about things here. In less than an hour, you'll see exactly what I'm talking about."

"See, as in another attack? If so, what's the point of launching a full-scale attack on a hidden village? What do we gain from something like that?"

"It wouldn't just be Azoco. It would be Tortuga, Cordela, and Sadeena. Everything leading up to this will be nothing compared to what happens next. The entire continent of Hasania itself will fall tonight."

"All of Hasania? How is that even possible? You would have to have thousands of machines to even—"

"There are over a hundred thousand Phantom-Bombers hidden throughout the regions ready to engage. Needless to say, numbers aren't an issue here. Now enough, we're leaving right now. Get ready to return to your Training Academy. We're heading back to where this all started."

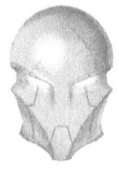

CHAPTER 12

October 3rd – 8:50PM

"5 6-0405, Agent David Fallon III reporting," he says, entering the Tortuga Forensics Headquarters. This was his third attempt, but no one from the security detail were responding. "That's pretty strange. It isn't like them not to answer their phones either. Maybe I should have had James join me after all," Agent Fallon thinks to himself as he inspects the entrances.

Having rushed to the location after receiving an ominous message, Agent Fallon is forced to push his brother's revelation aside.

After all, it is one thing to suggest Agent Keyes had a hand in creating the Phantom-Bombers, but it was another to supposedly receive a message from the dead man that same evening.

With so much to focus on, Agent Fallon didn't realize that it begun to rain. Rain has traditionally been a bad omen in Hasania, but, not being one for believing in such things, Agent Fallon decided not to pay that any mind.

"Great, just great. Well, there's no point of idly standing around here any longer," Agent Fallon said as he set a miniature electronic device on one of the side entrances. "Desperate times call for desperate measures, I suppose."

A small explosion destroyed the locks on the doors, allowing Agent Fallon into the facility. Once inside, he realized that the majority of rooms and hallways had little to no lighting.

While he initially thought that he was completely alone, a faint humming sound came from the distance. Trying not to draw any attention to himself, Agent Fallon slowly drew his sword as he stealthily maneuvered through the facility's corridors.

The rain began to intensify outside. At one point, the humming stopped, only for the sound of classical music to pour throughout the building, leaving a particularly haunting feeling.

Coming to the end of the main hall, Agent Fallon faces his main office. With the door slightly ajar, he cautiously made his way inside.

Surprised at seeing his office lit by two large candles on the opposite sides of the room, Agent Fallon sees an individual with their back toward him.

"Don't move! You have breached a LanTech Facilitation Building. I order you to identify yourself immediately," Agent Fallon demands. "If not, you will be met with appropriate force."

"While I appreciate you keeping to protocol, is that really how to address your Commanding Officer?"

Upon hearing his voice, Agent Fallon immediately recognized it as the leader of the LanTech Movement was standing in his office.

Whether it was the platinum blond hair, or unsettlingly deep gray eyes, the Commanding Officer's presence was undeniable.

"C-Commander Lansient? My apologies, Sir, but why? What are you doing out here?"

"Me? Off the record, it gets pretty tiring being away from everything going on. Seeing how you all have had quite the eventful series of events lately, I couldn't think of a better time to show my face," Commander Lansient replies, as he throws his black overcoat with its dark-red lining over a large desk chair.

"Well, Sir, there have been a series of chaotic moments as of late, but please rest assured that we are on top of things. We have the best and brightest on—"

"Lord…If you insist on being so gung-ho about things, then the least you could do is offer me a drink."

"Sir! I could never!"

"Fallon…"

"Tortuga Whiskey or Colonia Rum?" Agent Fallon asked in defeat. "For the record, these were gifts that I just so happened to leave here for decorative purposes."

"Yeah, sure. Rum it up, Fallon. Be sure to grab yourself something too!"

After grabbing a couple of glasses and some ice, Agent Fallon carefully prepared the drinks as directed. Commander Lansient raises his glass in approval as he begins to quietly enjoy his drink of choice.

Agent Fallon, on the other hand, sips cranberry juice, insisting that he feels more comfortable with that. A few minutes pass before Commander Lansient speaks.

"So, what've you got for me? Is there anything in particular on your mind?"

"Yes, Sir. Respectfully asking, but why exactly are you at this facility? That and is there any particular reason my staff members are not here?"

"And here I thought you were going to compliment me on the

lighting? I guess you aren't much for theatrics, after all. As far as your staff, I sent them home. As a leader, you should know not to work your people to the bone."

"Do you really stand by that, Sir?"

"Oh, definitely. Empathy, or at least the illusion of it, goes a long way. But between you and me, you get way more mileage out of them that way."

"N-noted, Sir. My team has put all of their effort into these recent events. Sir, I can honestly tell you that we have the best and brightest on—"

"Fallon, you're killing me here! Just for that, I want you to have a real drink to keep from stressing me out any further!"

"But, Sir—"

"Fine! If you want to play it that way, then consider that an order. Now get to it already."

"Truth be told, a drink or two would probably be for the best. I'm sure that you can agree that the world has been turned upside down lately."

"Well, it wouldn't be the first time. It's just a matter of adapting to things. Or was it evolving with time? Where did you say this rum was from again?"

"Sorry, but there is something I really need to know, Sir. I received an urgent message to come here, only to find you. Could you tell me what's really going on?"

"Oh, getting straight to business, I see. Fair enough. As I'm sure you are aware, Lawrence was more on the technological side compared to me when it comes to the Empire. He had a real affinity when it came to all of the airships and mechs we have today."

"Of course, Sir. He taught me just about everything that I know and even then, I'm probably at a fraction of his level on my best day."

"What he lacked, respectfully speaking, is common sense where it really mattered. For years, I would tell him that his technological advances could potentially be a problem if left unchecked."

"But what does that have to do with the message that I received from Agent Keyes?"

"A message from Keyes' device? It should be clear that it came from me."

"But, Sir, that simply isn't impossible. The authentications—"

"That was something I pressed Keyes to program, yes. But only on the grounds that I could override any protocol as the Commanding Officer."

"What would drive you to do that? Was it mistrust about Agent Keyes?"

"Trust? No, it has nothing to do with that. I can only trust anyone as far as I could throw them, as, in the world that we're living in, you can never be too careful. Case in point–Keyes is gone. The fact that I solely have a handle on our technology now means the Empire can continue to thrive in his wake."

"Don't you think that is too much power for one person to have? You have several Agents who you could delegate authorization to. Why not utilize us accordingly, Sir?"

"You are more like Keyes than you realize, Fallon. More times often than not, he felt the same way. Despite being older than me by quite a few years, I've been able to hold my own during our many debates. We had our disagreements, but we always kept things respectful as peers."

"But if you are willing to admit Agent Keyes' superior expertise when it came to technology, then where do your strengths come into play?"

"While the Empire is known for our machines, we wouldn't be

any different from anyone else without what I bring to the table: power. Without any clear purpose or direction, LanTech would have crumbled a long time ago. Keyes was essential, I'll say that much, but Hasania's prosperity is thanks to me."

"With all due respect, you're speaking as if the High Councils of Hasania don't play a part in this as well."

"Play a part? You know as well as I do that they're all puppets. Whether you're talking about Chambers, Balcer, or Young, they could all be easily replaced. They are only in their positions to keep the masses satisfied."

"I see. Empathy, or at least the illusion of it…"

"Exactly, Fallon. You've got play to politics here and there if you're in it for the long run. Isn't that a goal of yours in the first place or am I confusing you for your brother?"

"S-Sir!"

"Unlike your brother, you didn't disable the comms on your communication device. Even though I could only make out what some of you were saying, just know that your conversation from earlier won't leave this room."

"Okay, Sir. So, with that out in the open, could you tell me what this meeting is all about?"

"I've been monitoring the Keyes and Phantom investigations from a distance. Not to micromanage your operations, but I was curious to see where things would go with your generation taking the helm."

"But the fact that you're here…"

"Means that I've run out of patience. Don't take things personally. I believe most of you genuinely put your best efforts for the sake of the Empire. I appreciate the drive on that end. However, you all could only go so far without knowing the full picture."

"You mean that there's more to the investigation?"

"More than you could imagine, Fallon. There's no point in keeping you in the dark any longer: I've been well aware of Operation Phantom for years now."

"You can't be serious, Sir! Then, that means…"

"Yes, these machines were created by Agent Keyes. Operation Phantom was supposed to be his legacy. A means to minimize casualties on both sides and solidify the LanTech Empire as the driving force of peace in the world."

"Then what is the issue with such a project? Why hasn't it gotten off the ground?"

"Do you have brain damage or something? Minimizing casualties? Driving force of peace? We're not in the business of ending these constant battles; we thrive off of them."

"But, Sir, the LanTech Empire is—"

"Exactly what I order it to be, Agent. I'll let you in on something that I've had to get through Keyes' head again and again. The Empire isn't in the business to make friends. Nor do we operate for the needs of Hasania. We're here for one reason and one reason only: Order."

"You mean to tell me that we're here for something so simplistic?"

"Wake up, and take a look at the world around us right now, Fallon. Without the Empire, there would be nothing stopping those savages out there from burning everything to hell. They're basically animals compared to us and what we stand for."

"My apologies, but that's something that I simply cannot agree with, Sir."

"I beg your pardon? You seriously can't be so stubborn to resist our reality, can you? And here I thought you were one of the brighter Agents."

"To me, the Empire represents balance in the world. If we can't see that, then we're no different—"

"From the rest of them...Damn, son, it's like you are reading notes straight from Keyes' playbook. Let's put this to the side for now. Do you want to know the real reason why I'm here?"

"Of course, Sir. We've spent quite a bit of time talking around it, but I would really like to understand."

"Well, if you insist," Commander Lansient replies as he approaches his overcoat. "Do you care to explain what this is?"

Commander Lansient tosses a dark object towards Agent Fallon. To his shock, it is Varun's partially destroyed Phantom Helmet. He's confused why the Commanding Officer would possess this.

"Sir, where in the world did you get something like this? My team has only been able to retrieve small fragments here and there, but nothing like this."

"Well, it's a good thing that I have my own team on it, isn't it? Do you really think I would sit back and leave investigations like this in the hands of a few throwaway Agents?"

"Just what are you trying to say, Sir?"

"What I'm saying is that I've had Elite Agent Van looking into these recent events as well. Again, nothing personal or anything, but we have people in these positions for a reason. Anyway, she was able to uncover quite a few connections regarding everything that has been going on lately."

"Such as?"

"Well, the simple fact that, even though Operation Phantom was initiated by Keyes and scrapped by myself, someone still took it upon themselves to release waves of Phantoms without authorization."

"Well, then it is a simple case of rebels getting a hold of these machines."

"Clever theory, Fallon. But these machines could not be operated without an Agent's involvement. That was something I made clear to Keyes before the project fell through."

"I'll believe it when I see it, Sir. We've pledged unwavering loyalty to the Empire and I doubt that any of us would do anything to compromise what we stand for like this."

"I expect you'd say something like that. Sorry to break it to you, Agent, but the coding on these Phantoms have Agent James Fallon's name all over them."

"My brother?? Sir, there's absolutely no way!"

"I wouldn't imagine that there would be an easy way to hear this, but it is true. I had Agents Van and Connors analyze the data thoroughly. There is no denying that your brother has a hand in these recent attacks."

"Not him, not James...Sorry, but there has to be some kind of mistake. If I could just get the chance to review their findings, then maybe—"

"No, I won't let it happen. It is one thing for him to have a part in these acts, but for him to parade around as an integral asset to these investigations is particularly insulting to me. The fact that he approached you in the manner that he did should make this clear."

"I understand, Sir. There's no way of convincing you otherwise on this, but I have one request. Please let me be the one to bring him in."

"Denied, Fallon. While your dedication to the Empire is appreciated, there's no guarantee that your familial connection won't compromise things going forward."

"If he is backed into a corner, then there's no telling what he'll do with the Phantom Bombers that he has under his control. Is it really worth risking any collateral damage when attempting to bring him in?"

"If the reports are correct, then there isn't much time before the next attack happens. So, regardless, large scale destruction is inevitable at this rate. If it means anything to you, I didn't want it to go this way. But given the circumstances…"

"No need to explain yourself, Sir. If it's meant to be, then it's—"

Agent Fallon's words are cut short as a major explosion obliterates the Tortuga Forensics Building.

This explosion has the combined effect of causing an electromagnetic disturbance, sending Tortuga and the rest of Hasania into complete and utter darkness.

Several airships lose their power mid-flight, causing many of them to crash into buildings throughout major cities.

The violent flames from the wreckage were the only sources of light until ominous blue beams appeared throughout Hasania.

The sense of dread is felt all the way over in the Azoco village where Lady Aida looks into the distance.

Requesting that the villagers prepare more torches in spite of the ongoing rainfall, she signals for silence as unknown forces make their way through the forest.

"I can tell there is a group making their way towards the village, but I can't sense their presence. Could they be more of those machines?" Lady Aida thinks to herself.

Heavy footsteps grew louder so Lady Aida realized that the invaders were surrounding the village.

Knowing that there was no time to spare, Lady Aida requested Weiss to lead the villagers to their homes.

Reacting to the sound of her voice, a horde of Phantoms suddenly lunge towards the village elder at an aggressive rate.

Drawing various blades and spears, they clearly intended to immediately execute Lady Aida, before being frozen in place out of seemingly nowhere.

This group of Phantoms was promptly set ablaze, while their reinforcements were halted by a large wall made of wood and stone.

As Lady Aida gave her thanks, the group of warriors made their way toward her.

"I thought the plan was for me to take advantage of all this rain by freezing the Bombers? Work smarter, not harder, you idiot!"

"Yeah, whatever! Your way was taking too long! Besides there's a ton of them out there, so you'll have chances to go at it again and again. Let's not forget who is running the show, Icebox!"

"Lord Haden, if you could hear me right now, all I ask is that you give me the strength to deal with these two during all of this."

"Look sharp, everyone," Benjamin says. "If we slip up, then this village is done for. It's either us or these bastards, so let's make it an easy choice from here, shall we?"

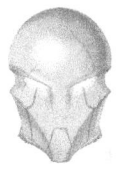

CHAPTER 13

*U*rgent message: This is not a drill; again, this is not a drill. It has been recently confirmed that the explosion that recently decimated the Tortuga Forensics Facility claimed the life of Commander Drake Lansient.

In addition to this, sightings of rogue militias have been reported throughout Hasania.

Effective immediately, a Full-Force Order is hereby directed. All LanTech Agents and Officials are to engage any and all unknown individuals with deadly force.

Again, if you encounter any non-member of the LanTech Empire, you are ordered to eliminate them at all costs.

Released: B. Alteme, Acting Commander of the LanTech Empire.

"If the Forensics Facility was destroyed, then that means my brother—"

"Sir, is everything alright," Paul asks a clearly distraught Agent Fallon. "Does that message affect our mission in any way?"

"No, we'll still press on. Either way, we're coming up on the Training

Academy. Though by the looks of things, calling it the Academy Ruins seems much more appropriate."

The full moon shines on their destination as Agent Fallon and Paul approach the broken-down remnants of where the Training Academy once proudly stood.

Rain has clearly made its way through the massive holes on roofs and ceilings, further adding to the gloom.

There was a ghostly silence where thousands of trainees and instructors once spent hours upon hours preparing for the years ahead of them.

Sadly, there was no future for the individuals who did not survive the attack; just a hushed stillness among a sea of debris.

"You are awfully quiet all of a sudden, Fehren. You aren't getting nostalgic about this place, are you?"

"No, not at all. The time that I have spent here is long behind me. The only thing that matters now is helping you fulfill your true objective, Sir."

"Ah, good answer. Very well, Fehren. Let's keep making our way through the main building. You will be able to understand more about what's going on shortly."

"Is that really for the best? After all, most of the Academy has been destroyed. I wouldn't imagine that there would be much to work with anymore."

"I guess it makes sense for you to say that seeing how you don't know the big picture. Well, listen up. Now's the best time for you to know about The Metallic Siege."

"The Metallic Siege, Sir?"

"Yes. About five years ago, I was a merchant marine that occasionally worked alongside the Empire. I wasn't a standout by any means, but all that mattered was that I was competent at my job."

"Is that when all of this started, Sir?"

"Maybe, I'm not sure. One night, I was on one of the security watches on one of our smaller ships when we were attacked by a rebel ship off of the Northern Tortugan Shores. Going against them was like bringing a knife to a sword fight. There wasn't much of a guarantee that we would be able to fend them off."

"What ended up happening that night?"

"I did what any other young, dumb person would do in that situation. I went all in and made the decision to board their ship. I figured if they were so hard pressed on getting our ship, they wouldn't be as focused on protecting theirs."

"If I didn't know any better, it sounded like you went off on a suicide mission."

"Hey now. If you haven't been in that kind of position before, then you probably wouldn't understand. Worst case scenario, the rebels were going to kill me anyway. I figured I wouldn't give those guys the satisfaction."

"Well, when you put it like that…"

"Exactly. Anyway, when I boarded their ship, I noticed that they barely had enough people to man the thing. My guess was that they were planning on using our sailors to help make their escape."

"But what would they be escaping from?"

"That ship of theirs was not one you would ever want to be on. It was loaded with tons of explosives. More than most rebels would ever be able to get a hold of, even off of the black market. The bombs were slated to explode once the ship reached a specific set of coordinates: Tortuga Capital City."

"Why did they plan on attacking there of all places? What were they hoping to accomplish by doing that?"

"I didn't know and didn't care. All I knew was that if I didn't act on things, a lot of people would end up dead. Fighting off the rebels was pretty much out of the question because they overpowered us by a long shot."

"I decided to reprogram their detonation mechanism by rewriting their expected coordinates to a location in the middle of the sea."

"You mean to tell me that you did all of that instead of trying to find a way out of there? What were you hoping to accomplish with all of this?"

"Huh, are you even listening? It wasn't about me from then on. If I didn't do something—anything—about the situation, then things would really go south. I was able to escape by the time the rebels figured out what was going, but, by then, the explosions destroyed their ship."

"That means you ended up being a hero. And that has to do with The Metallic Siege how?"

"By the time I recovered, I found out I was being charged with counts of capital murder. Apparently, there were two Agents working undercover aboard their vessel that night. They were posing as rebels for months and their plan was to gather more intel on how these warriors were able to arm themselves with explosives of that caliber."

"But there were more than just explosives, weren't there?"

"Now you're starting to see where this all connects. In addition to the explosives, there were prototypes for mechs that I've never seen before. Between the advanced armor and sensors, something told me that if rebels were to use these, battles between them and LanTech would never be the same. It probably would have sparked a war that would end up destroying the world as we know it."

"Why didn't you just explain that your actions were done for the sake of protecting Tortuga? Surely someone would understand where you were coming from."

"No one wanted to draw attention to the fact that LanTech was aware of this machinery. They feared that other rebels with that technology would strike once word of these mechs got out. The safest bet was to execute me as soon as possible to avoid any potential conflicts. My fate was sealed until someone stepped up to defend me: Agent Keyes."

"Agent Keyes? Why would a Senior Agent go out of their way for your sake?"

"His words were that I displayed acts of courage in the face of an imminent threat towards Tortuga and Hasania as a whole. Using his influence, my charges were not only dropped, but I received an offer to commission as a LanTech Agent a few weeks later."

"I'm sorry, but I still don't understand why someone on his level would take such a leap of faith."

"Neither did I, at least not at first. But not too long after I officially became an Agent, he revealed to me the truth behind those machines. How they were supposed to be his greatest gift to the world, but, in his words, he believed that we weren't ready for their greatness."

"So, Agent Keyes really was the one behind all of this?"

"Yes, and no. You see, Agent Keyes believed by empowering the Empire with these machines, then the rebels throughout the regions would naturally end their side of the conflict. I believed that LanTech utilizing these machines would only make things worse."

"Then why were the machines in the dark for so many years?"

"Despite his seniority, the late Commander Drake and members of the Executive Council denied Keyes the authorization to deploy them. After the incident that got me involved in the first place, they didn't want to run the risk of rebels gaining access to the machines for their own use."

"Okay, you just decided to use the machines on your own once Keyes died?"

"No, that's not it. Earlier this year, a number of these machines went missing. Agent Keyes and I were more or less the only ones who knew their true destructive capabilities."

"I don't get it...Why didn't you just utilize the Empire to track down the machines?"

"That wasn't an option. It was only a matter of time before information got out that Agent Keyes created them. That type of knowledge about a senior Agent would irretrievably tarnish the Empire. He took it upon himself to go on an op with the goal of destroying the missing machines."

"But on August 30th..."

"Yes, Fehren. That was the day he was killed. It seemed as though rebels got the best of him. By the time I was able to head to our main labs, I saw that an attack was slated for this Academy and another one for Prospear Bridge as well."

"If you knew this much, why didn't you try stopping them?"

"I couldn't even if I wanted to. The protocols were designed by Agent Keyes so that only he could rewrite them. The attacks were inevitable. All I could do was retrieve as much data as I could in an attempt to stay steps ahead."

"What ended up happening to the ones who killed Keyes?"

"I believe they were wiped out during the attack on Prospear. I'm sure that you've noticed that there hasn't been a Phantom Strike since then, haven't you? I've been spending my time up until now trying to override Keyes' protocols. You should know that the little skirmish in

Azoco going south didn't exactly help things either."

"I could understand you wanting to retrieve the Phantom in that village, but why were you so determined to go after Keenth? What does he have to do with all of this?"

"Agent Keyes pulled data from LanTech's databases to form reports for his projects. Your friend was among the many names listed as a Person of Interest. While the reasons behind them being listed varied, I know that Hedstrom's exceptional potential was something worth looking into."

"But how did I get involved, Sir? Was I recognized as one as well?"

"No, you weren't. Unfortunately, your role in all of this was a rather simple one– you were a means to get a hold of Hedstrom. When the attack took place here, my goal was to retrieve him. He was able to escape somehow, so I decided to utilize you."

"Then these enhancements?"

"They're modified versions of the technology used with the Phantoms. After all, you wouldn't be much use to me if you couldn't hold your own out there."

"I understand. One final question, Sir: why are we standing around these ruins, instead of the labs that you mentioned?"

"I'm sure you've heard that Agent Keyes helped establish the Training Academy. But what people didn't realize was that he was a pretty sentimental guy. This place is somewhere that he held at a high regard."

"W-wait...You mean if he was to have secret labs—"

"Then they would be hiding in plain sight," Agent Fallon states as he raises his right arm, causing the ground before them to tremble. To Paul's surprise, several rows of Phantom-Bombers rise in unison.

"And that's The Metallic Siege," Agent Fallon explains. "While his intentions may have been in the right place, Agent Keyes was stuck in the past. The nonstop fighting between LanTech and the rebels won't end until they wake up and find a common goal."

"Then by releasing these Phantoms—"

"They'll have no choice, but to be humbled by the machines and their power. People would finally use their potential in this world as they were put here for. They may not understand it, but I do. And if doing all of this takes me being seen as a monster, then so be it. This is something that I've already made peace with."

"That's good, it really is. I'm glad that you are content with your decision."

"Really? Now why would you say that, Fehren?"

"So that you can die with no regrets," Paul angrily replies as he swings his sword at Agent Fallon.

"Are you out of your goddamn mind," Agent Fallon shouts, feeling a laceration on the left side of his face. "What the hell do you think you're doing?"

"Just something that I should have done a long time ago, Fallon. You'll regret trying to use someone like me as your puppet," Paul continues as he rips the defunct slave crown from his head. "I'm ending this here and now!"

"That's a pretty bold claim, kid. Still, words will only get you so far," Agent Fallon announces as he summons a Phantom to engage Paul. "I should have taken you out while I had the—"

"Too slow," Paul replies, having instantly bifurcated the machine before Agent Fallon could react. "Thanks for the enhancements, by the way. If you want anyone to blame for this, then start with yourself."

"You act as if working on your enhancements was the only project to my name," Agent Fallon states as a massive machine emerges from the ground.

Paul stands, shocked at the menacing foe towering before him.

"You seem surprised? Do you really think I would go on with this crusade without planning accordingly? These Phantoms are connected to one another and use a unique energy source. An energy source powerful enough to be unaffected by EMPs like the one from earlier."

"So, then this thing…?"

"Yes, I decided to design a machine to ensure that nothing stands in my way. Fehren, this is the Omega Phantom. Say what you want, but I felt it was only right to let you know what ended up killing you in the end."

The Omega Phantom reveals several blade-like claws, before rushing toward Paul. Despite its size, the Omega could uses its unbelievable speed to attack its opponent.

A direct strike on the Omega from Paul's sword was surprisingly ineffective, seeing how his weapon was believed to be powerful enough to cut through practically anything.

After narrowly dodging a counterattack, Paul decided to use the knowledge of the Academy's corridors to his advantage.

But then the Omega releases an array of explosives that incapacitate Paul. Looming over him, the Omega begins to charge up to deliver a massive blast to end the battle.

Paul quickly throws his sword towards the Omega, only for the machine to dodge the attack. The Omega continues to charge its attack, while Agent Fallon joins in to give Paul a fitting send off.

"You only have yourself to blame, Fehren. Slumped over there, unarmed, only to die like an animal. You should have just shut up and stayed in your place," Agent Fallon taunts. "He really needs to work on that habit of speaking too soon…Wouldn't you agree, Keenth!"

Before Agent Fallon can react, the Omega Phantom is swiftly

destroyed by being impaled by two swords.

Moving himself away from its subsequent explosion, Agent Fallon is furious at the seeing Paul standing alongside the newly arrived Keenth Hedstrom.

"Hey, it took you long enough, man!"

"Yeah, yeah. Better late than never. Besides, I wouldn't need to rush if you would have just handled Fallon and these machines on your own, now would I?"

"Sure, whatever. But seriously Keenth, about before…"

"What about it? I ran into Richard on the way here and he explained what he could. What happened in Azoco wasn't your fault. I don't blame you for anything."

"You can't be serious?"

"Yeah, I mean it. I'm not going to hold you up over stuff like that. The one thing that matters right now is stopping Fallon, once and for all," Keenth says. "The only question is whether you're with me on this or not, Paul?"

"Ha! Isn't it obvious," Paul replies. "Let's go all out in crushing this guy, Keenth!"

"You two, stopping me? There's no way you fools are serious about that," Agent Fallon said looking down on his opponents from a banister. "I've come too far with all of this to be defeated now."

"The show's gotta end sometime, Fallon. Unfortunately for you, your time ends with us," Keenth replies as he tosses Paul back his sword in preparation for battle.

"Attempting to take me down won't change anything. Not with LanTech, not with the rebels, and not with Hasania at all. You know that the endless cycle will just go on and on! Why are you resisting my plan to change all of that?"

"Because that plan of yours takes the ability to choose away from people," Keenth replies. "This world isn't perfect, but a plan like yours is nothing to live for. If anything, it would just be a reflection of you and your beliefs."

"Oh, so you know what I believe in all of a sudden? Feel free to enlighten me, Hedstrom!"

"Fear. This little plan of yours is grounded in fear and fear alone. Fear of having no purpose in this world, aside from dying as part of a collective cause. This was never about LanTech or the rebels, was it? You're just afraid that your existence has and will never amount to anything in the large scheme of things. Tell me I'm wrong, Fallon!"

"Bwahahaha," Agent Fallon cackles. "No, I can't! I can't because you are absolutely right with that one! The thought of dying a mediocre death haunts me more than I could ever put into words!"

"We've all gotta go sometime and if I know it's my time, then I'll do everything in my power to make sure I die with a purpose," Agent Fallon declares as he raises his Auraen erratically for battle.

As he finally draws his sword, Agent Fallon is abruptly stabbed from behind. Keenth and Paul stare as a torrent of blood continues to drench an unknown blade.

Agent Fallon struggles to turn around, only to see what appears to be a Phantom-Bomber draped in a black-hooded cloak.

The assailant removes their sword from Agent Fallon, only for him to fall on his knees.

"If death is what you seek, then allow me to fulfill that desire," a voice replies.

"…T-that voice…Not you…Anyone, but you, David…"

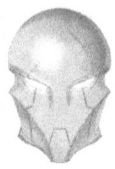

CHAPTER 14

"Yo, just keep 'em coming! I could tear through these freaks all day," Benjamin vigorously announces after using a wave of Efir to destroy a swarm of Phantoms. "You two better start pulling your own weight too!"

"Isn't it a little too late into the battle to say something like that," Beth responds as she forms a large ice shield over her left arm. "Besides, don't you have anything better to do than make a competition out of this?"

"That's no way to talk to your superior, Beth! If I didn't know any better, I would say that you've gotten pretty lazy over these past couple of weeks. I wouldn't take you as someone who would fall off so—Wait, did you just freeze my leg?"

"Are you sure that was me? Wow, it looks like I've gotten a bit rusty, after all," Beth replies. "You should probably get that looked at soon. After all, I would hate to hear that you ended up with permanent damage or something."

"Like hell I would! A block of ice like this is nothing to me! I'll burn this village down just to thaw it out before I'd let something like this—"

"Let's not get too comfortable, buddy!"

Benjamin is swatted aside several feet by an unknown individual. Before he can retaliate, Cory calls out.

"Kendra! It is so great to have you back!"

"Yeah, yeah. Hold your applause folks, Mama Kendra has returned! This is probably the part where I thank some of you for holding down the fort, but…"

"You've chosen the quintessential setting to die," Benjamin blurts. "Is that any way to acknowledge the person who's single-handedly defending Azoco?"

"Says the person who just threatened to burn MY village down! And what the hell is this about 'single-handedly'? You're literally fighting alongside two very capable—sorry, hang on a second—"

Kendra surrounds her right arm with Reiki Auraen and unleashes a wave of energy to soundly obliterate a dozen Phantoms.

"My bad. Alright now, where were we?"

"You know what, I think we're good over here. I think I'm going to go ahead and back up Cory with the, you know, fighting stuff that we've got going on. Cool? Cool."

"Sounds good to me. Still, I thought Keenth would be here too. I guess he ended up defeating Kusari before I got the chance to fight her again."

"W-wait? You two have thrown hands with Kusari and lived to tell about it? And you mean to tell me that Keenth actually surpassed her?"

"You shouldn't sound so surprised, guy. He's gotten strong. Really strong. It looks like we ended up making a man out of him, after all."

"But for him to get that powerful as fast as he did is insane! What the hell were you feeding him anyway?"

"I don't know, mostly stir-fry probably? Anyway, let's quit yapping around! If you really want to see the strength of Azoco, then pay attention!"

"It's time to get rid of the trash looking to destroy our village, once and for all," Kendra exclaims as she powers up to Reiki Mode, only for the energy to dissipate.

"I mean...That looked cool and all, but...," Benjamin thinks as the secondhand embarrassment begins to set in.

"But how? How is this even possible?"

"It's because your strength hasn't fully recovered," Lady Aida explains. "You shouldn't push yourself like this. I'm sure Lord Haden did his best given the little time he had, but it'll take a while for your Auraen to return to its normal levels."

"Sorry, but time isn't exactly a luxury right now! There's only so much the four of us can do to defend the village before..." Kendra shudders, sensing a tremendous amount of Auraen in the distance.

"You feel, don't you? This presence has to be—"

"Keenth...There's no doubt that it's Keenth's. But for us to feel it from all the way out here...What in the world is he up against right now?"

"Well, I'd imagine that the best way to answer that question is to see for yourself, Kendra."

"Me? I don't have the strength or means to do it."

"The crystal I used to send you and Keenth off to Haden finally cracked when I summoned the others to Azoco. It has just enough power to send you. If anyone should be by his side right now, I know it should be you. Just leave the village to us and help end the real battle, Kendra!"

"Okay, you've got it!"

*

October 3rd – 9:30 PM

"Did he say 'David'? As in his brother? But he was killed at the Forensics Building," Paul says. "This just doesn't make any sense…"

"It is simply a matter beyond your comprehension," David replies, lifting his jet-black hood as he continues forward.

His appearance, now in full view, is an intricate version of the Phantom-Bomber Armor, equipped with a variety of explosives on his side.

Discarding his signature glasses, David stares down Keenth and Paul. Before they can question him, James rises to his feet in an attempt to confront his brother.

"W-what the hell is going on? With that explosion, y-you shouldn't be alive."

"That's a pretty ironic thing for you to say, all things considered. Regardless, it would take a lot more than that to kill me. Everything fell right into place, as expected."

"Shut the hell up! You're spouting nonsense as if you were in on any of this!"

"If you weren't so ignorant, then you'd be able to see that you were being led along this whole time. If you stop and think about it, do you really think a horde of machines of this level would be entrusted to someone like you?"

"Of course, they were! Agent Keyes and I were the only ones involved with Operation Phantom! There's no way that anyone else—"

"Surely you didn't honestly believe that encountering the rebel vessel years ago was all a stroke of luck, right? How pitiful. The two

Agents that were on an undercover mission were on the verge of exposing the operation. Eliminating them inspired us to integrate you into our true intentions."

"Our? You don't mean—"

"Agent Keyes and myself, of course. Operation Phantom was our endgame the whole time. When it came to getting the project off of the ground, I proposed bringing you into the fold."

"So, you're saying that you people used me…"

"Don't speak regretfully. You served your purpose, James. While you clearly aren't as technologically proficient as Keyes or myself, you were capable enough to play your part."

"Did this process include killing Keyes too?"

"Killing Keyes was a necessity. He was too stuck playing politics to get our machines off of the ground. At the end of the day, he wouldn't budge when it came to deploying the Phantoms for the sake of the Empire."

"Look at you! You speak as if you aren't doing the same, David!"

"A conclusion like that shows why you are such a fool, James. Do you really think I would dedicate so much time and effort to benefit LanTech? There was something that the recently deceased commander shared with me that I partially agree with."

"It was probably a lovely conversation, I'm sure."

"Most of the beings who roam Hasania are truly animals. Dirty, filthy animals driven only by their instincts and personal self-interests. In his arrogance, Lansient didn't realize that I detest LanTech all the same."

"That means your goal was never to use the Phantoms for the sake of LanTech's dominance, was it?"

"I could never lower myself to such blind allegiance. LanTech's rhetoric is just as toxic as the rest of the beasts in Hasania. It should be clear that this world isn't even worth salvaging. By wiping out all opposition, nothing will stand in my way from reshaping Hasania according to my vision."

"You call me arrogant, yet you speak as if you're a god? You're sick, David."

"Mind your tongue, James. You barely have enough strength to remain standing. You'll just end up shortening your lifespan further if you make the mistake of pushing me, brother."

"I'd rather die than consider a psychopath like you my—"

"Pity," David states as he slashes James across the chest. "I can only be so merciful; I'm not one to be tested, James. I've come too far for this to be proven otherwise."

As James falls down, David begins his descent to Keenth and Paul.

Upon reaching them, the colossal waves of energy that emit from David's armor begin to rock the Academy Ruins. Keenth and Paul respond by raising their respective Auraens.

"I take it that I'm supposed to be impressed by this," David states. "Perhaps you think that if you were able to destroy the Omega Phantom and the inferior models that you have a chance against me?"

"I guess we'll just have to find out," Keenth responds. "There's no better time than right now."

"I see. You may regret hearing this, but the Omega was a machine of James' making. Unsurprisingly, he thought he was the first to come to the conclusion of making advancements on the Phantom-Bomber models."

"Is that your way of saying that what you have stands above that?"

"The question you should really be asking is what is an Omega to an Alpha like me," David replies, as he dons his advanced Phantom Mask. "Though I'm afraid the path to reaching that answer will be quite painful."

"…Paul, there's a quick change of plan," Keenth states as he observes David's power continuing to increase. "Grab James and get as far away as possible on the airship you got here with."

"Are you out of your mind, Keenth? What do we possibly have to gain from saving Fallon?"

"There's no telling where the rest of the machines are. If we can get Fallon to say where they are and how to possibly decommission them altogether, then it's worth looking into after I end this battle."

"You might be right, but there's no way that you can do this alone!"

"That's the thing, Paul. One way or another, this all ends tonight."

"After you end this battle? You're here to take me down? You truly must have gone mad," David responds. "I'll allow it; I wouldn't want any interference while I take my time to terminate you."

"Ah, because I'm a Person of Interest or something?"

"Hardly. To you, this will be the final fight of your life. For me? Killing you off here will be just an afterthought," David announces as he draws his metal rapier. "It is fitting that your journey in Hasania began and will shortly end here."

Instead of answering David, Keenth glances over at Paul who responds with a nod, before moving towards James Fallon's location.

"I'm disgusted at the thought of someone like you being so highly affiliated with the LanTech Empire. You bring nothing, but shame to their name, David."

"LanTech was only a means to reach my true goals. No more, no less."

"Whatever, say what you have to convince yourself otherwise. Do you mean to tell me that these goals included killing your brother?"

"What can I say? I can adapt to circumstances. How does that affect you in the slightest? Isn't James your enemy?"

"That's beside the point. Something about you hurting your own brother doesn't sit well with me, David."

"Again, I fail to see how this matters to you in the slightest. Stop referring to me as David. Agent David Fallon III died earlier, remember? All that remains now is the Alpha Phantom!"

"David, Fallon, Alpha...It doesn't matter to me what you call yourself. Somehow you survived death the first time, but I'll see to it that doesn't happen again!"

Keenth soars toward him and their blades clash at long last. His opponent strikes back, the stone structures of the Academy Ruins cracking under the pressure.

Increasing his Auraen to maneuver around the battlefield, Keenth carefully analyzes his opponent to use any openings to land a clear hit. To his shock, Fallon uses energy boosters to bombard Keenth with a series of blows.

While Keenth is able to defend himself from the successive attacks, he finds himself with only fractions of a second to collect himself.

It appears that the acclaim behind the Alpha Phantom Model wasn't all talk and this machine was leagues above any of the others that came before it.

Keenth did not allow the seemingly insurmountable odds deter him from defeating his opponent though. Releasing a torrent of Auraen, Fallon remains seemingly unfazed, only to realize that Keenth's sword strikes have increased considerably.

"So, he released his Auraen, only to re-absorb it with his sword,"

Fallon thinks to himself. "For him to skillfully utilize abilities at this level in such a short amount of time...It's beginning to make sense now..."

"Before we continue this, there's something that you must know," Fallon explains, as he creates a distance between Keenth and himself. "It is something that I'm sure is still crossing your mind."

"Humor me, Fallon. What is it?"

"Do you really want to know how I actually survived the explosion from earlier? I'm sure it would be useful to know what kind of abilities I have, after all."

"I don't know. I figured that you were probably using your Bombers somehow."

"The true power with the Phantoms is their sheer strength in numbers. The fact that you were able to combat them back on the bridge should make that point clear. Even you should understand that Phantoms wouldn't be able to withstand an attack of that magnitude."

"Then what did you end up doing?"

"Surely, you of all people should know," Fallon responds as he reveals a crystal necklace. "I take it that this looks familiar to you, Keenth?"

"W-wait, what? How did you end up with one of those?"

"I sincerely hope that you don't believe you are the only one capable of embarking on paths of enlightenment, are you? Did it ever cross your mind that there are others out there with exceptional potential as well?"

"Potential...Potential...Wait! You're not saying..."

"My ancestors were exiled from Azoco many years ago. Generations of my relatives went on to live as nomads throughout Hasania. People envied our latent abilities, but since we didn't know how to utilize them properly, many of us were killed off as time went on."

"Liar! That isn't something that Lady Aida or the others would allow to happen?"

"Yet here I stand before you having survived the odds. Years before I joined LanTech, I went on a path to truly harness my power. That's when I came across someone. A figure who provided you the means to finally harness true power."

"Sage Haden?"

"Yes, but not Haden. Did you really think there is only one way to gain this power. Unlike you, however, I was turned away. From there, I opted to kill the Sage and gain awakening by force. Doing this nearly left me dead. But, as you see, I lived on with the sole purpose revealing the world for what it truly is."

"So, you're the reason why Sage Haden was so hesitant in interfering with what's been going on in Hasania…"

"The Sages are nothing but cowards! I'm sure they know by now that my abilities have surpassed theirs because I was willing to evolve. There's a clear reason why I dedicated myself towards Operation Phantom."

"Was it because no one else would be crazy enough to join your cause?"

"No, that type of logic is beneath me. The real reason is because, as living beings, we all have limits. I don't care whether you are a human or even a Sage, there are understood limits and boundaries involved when it comes to flesh and bone."

"This talk about evolving is your way of saying you've surpassed the rest of us?"

"It should be abundantly clear that I have. I'm sure that you've noticed by now that you had an uphill battle on Prospear due to your strength eventually declining. The same will be seen with your allies fighting in Azoco village as we speak."

"If striking you down is all it takes to stop them from being defeated, then—"

"Don't speak as if you are exempt from this inevitably as well," Fallon retorts, swinging down on Keenth. "Did you really think that exerting your Auraen throughout our battle, would end in your favor?"

"Damn, he's right," Keenth thinks to himself as his breathing begins to become more difficult. "It doesn't seem like Fallon is having any problems at all."

"It seems as though you still don't understand, Keenth. Here, I want you to strike me. Right here, right now. Use all of your strength and I'll prove that you still won't be able to even scratch my armor."

"Tsh, maybe surviving death has made you even more arrogant, but it'll be my pleasure to finally take you out of your misery!"

Keenth pours the entirety of his Auraen into his sword and uses all of his strength to stab Fallon straight through the chest. This shatters the remaining windows in the vicinity of their battle.

To his shock and horror, Keenth looks up to see Fallon standing before him while half of his sword falls to the ground. Before Keenth can even comprehend what just happened, he is blasted through the shoulder.

"How...How in the hell," Keenth asks as he leaps away from his opponent. "That didn't come from his sword, did it?"

"With your recent increase in strength, the odds of you being able to contend with me in battle were a bit too high for my liking. That's why I designed this electromagnetic crossbow as a precaution."

"This isn't good," Keenth thinks to himself as he struggles to prepare a defense. "I can't afford to keep getting struck by these. A few more direct hits and—"

"Sure, this weapon is effective," Fallon taunts. "But it truly lacks the satisfaction of directly slaughtering opponents. No worries, I'm sure I'll just get over it."

Fallon maniacally fires a series of blasts towards Keenth who is barely able to dodge them. Keenth attempts to hide among his surroundings, but his wound makes him easy prey.

Seeing the opportunity to take a clear shot, Fallon prepares an enhanced blast to kill Keenth with one shot, but he's met with a sudden sword attack. He's confused since Keenth's blade was broken in two and it's a black blade which entered the fray.

"P-Paul! What are you doing here?"

"Finishing what we started! We have to stop this Fallon guy, now or never," Paul shouts back, as he continues battling.

"Funny, I didn't expect to be challenged by the help, of all people. Clearly, you coming back here means you could not wait to die. If you that is what you want so badly, then—"

Paul takes the opportunity to punch Fallon across the face. Revving up the brace around his arm, he attempts to do this again, but is stopped when his opponent grabs his wrist.

"While your strength is commendable, do you really think it could come anywhere close to mine?" Fallon boasts as he snaps Paul's arm in half. "You really must be determined to die in this Academy, after all."

"Don't you dare," Keenth frantically shouts as he wields what's left of his sword like a dagger. Before he can land a blow on the back of Fallon's neck, his opponent fires a blast at breakneck speed, hurdling Keenth back several feet away.

"Up until now, these blasts were simply designed to injure you. Killing you instantly would be terribly satisfying on my end, but alas, this skirmish must come to an end."

"Keenth Hedstrom," he continues. "Taking your life will hold more meaning than you realize. For some reason, you represent hope among these fools. But by hindering your light, I will not only break their bodies, but their spirits as well."

Fallon raises his arm towards Keenth as the Academy Ruins completely darken, only to be illuminated with the murderous glow of the energy blast he's formulating. Keenth makes inaudible pleas for his body to move, but to no avail.

Seeing that Keenth is completely incapacitated, the former Agent decides to impart his final words to his young opponent.

"You should be proud of your accomplishments, Hedstrom. Having survived against the Phantoms and Kusari, among other challenges. Had you gone against anyone aside from me, I'm sure you would have risen as the victor. Be sure to give Keyes my regards."

With those words, Fallon releases a mammoth of a blast that encompasses their entire battleground.

The fallout from the attack is so powerful that parts of the roof crash down in the surrounding area.

Fallon begins to walk away as the smoke and debris disperses. He stops himself from leaving the area after hearing labored breathing from a distance.

"No...No, not you. No...Why would you do that?"

Fallon focuses his attention on the aftermath of his blast. A bloodied warrior stands facing ahead, while their ally mourns.

"Come on, you've gotta say something...Anything at all," Keenth calls out. "Just give me something to know that you're okay, Paul..."

"S-sorry. I can't do it this time," Paul replies as he collapses onto the ground. "I think this just might be it for me, Keenth."

"But why...Why you? Why would you do this?" Keenth asks, while tightly holding onto his friend in an attempt to keep him conscious. "There was no reason to do that for me..."

"As much as I hate to admit it, the bastard is right about you. You do represent hope...Hope for a lot of us, including me...Now unless you want anyone else you care about to end up like me...Then you take my sword...my Fehrenblade...to defend Hasania from him...Do it, Keenth...Do it..."

"Apparently that blast wasn't enough. Fine, I'll use my blade properly to—"

Fallon is interrupted by Keenth's Auraen erupting throughout the Academy Ruins.

With his eyes filled with determination, Keenth arms himself with the sword of his fallen ally to conclude the battle once and for all.

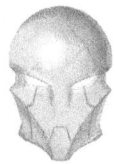

CHAPTER 15

"His strength...My sensors can barely process how much his power is increasing," Fallon thinks to himself. "Is this what Keyes was so cautious about?"

"Fallon, this is not the time for you to be distracted," Keenth informs him, as his Auraen continues to flare throughout the Academy Ruins. "I'll make you pay for what you did to Paul, even if it's the last thing I do!"

"Is that really the wisest thing to say? After all, that attack was intended for you. If anything, you only have yourself to blame for his death."

"He had a name and it was Paul Fehren," Keenth announces. "Now, say his name, Fallon."

"And if I refuse," Fallon mocks. "What will you do about it?"

Keenth vanishes from his opponent's sights, only to reappear several feet behind him. As Fallon turns to Keenth, a pool of blood is seen beneath his boots.

"Consider that as your only warning," Keenth taunts. "I'll be sure to actually cut off your arm this time the next time I attack you."

"Tsh...As if you'll have the opportunity to do that again!"

Fallon furiously unleashes a barrage of blasts, only for Keenth to dodge them all with little difficulty.

Realizing that Keenth's strength and stamina were no longer dwindling, Fallon doubts whether or not he will be able to defeat him after all.

"Him surpassing me is completely out of the question," Fallon thinks to himself. "A lowly savage like Hedstrom could never compare to my power."

"Hit me, Fallon."

"What's this foolish nonsense you speak of?"

"I'm serious, Fallon. I'm returning the favor by giving you the same opportunity that you gave me. Fire a blast directly at me. Right here, right now. Even with all of your strength, I'll prove that you—"

Fallon abruptly fires a direct shot at his opponent. Keenth holds back the blast with his bare hand and launches an attack at Fallon.

However, the blast didn't reach its intended target as Fallon led a band of Phantoms to serve as shields.

"The Metallic Siege is led by my hand and my hand alone," Fallon says, as he summons an arsenal of Phantoms. "I don't care what type of power you think you have, there's simply no way that you could defeat all of these while dealing with me!"

Keenth dashes forward, only for a mech to engage him. He grabs the Phantom by the neck and exerts his Auraen to the point where the entirety of Fallon's machines combust.

"You made mention of sensors, didn't you? Do you really think that your little puppets would be a match for me anymore? Do you even have any shame left?"

Keenth winces in pain from the injuries that he has endured.

"There's a reason why I didn't solely rely on the path to enhance my strength. It is clearly a short-term method. Too much power would simply destroy inexperienced entities. But by combing it with the technology to my disposal, I can bypass such restrictions."

"Oh, really? How do you explain me almost chopping your arm off?" Keenth confidently retorts. "This doesn't change anything. All I have to do is focus on finishing this quickly."

"You won't get the opportunity to," Fallon proclaims as he aims several blasts at the roof above Keenth. "It is a simple matter of draining and killing you!"

"Damn, he's right about that," Keenth thinks to himself as he dodges the falling debris. "It feels like my body is breaking under the pressure of all of this Auraen. But if I let my guard down, then I'll be defenseless to his attacks."

Keenth attempts to engage Fallon, but his foe is adamant in following through with his strategy. Seeing Fallon aiming at Paul's body, Keenth rushes forward and takes a direct hit through his stomach.

"No! That's the last thing that I need right now," Keenth screams, while applying pressure to his wound. "I really have no choice, but to focus my power on striking him down once and for—"

Keenth stumbles, but catches himself before he falls to the ground. Fallon fires a storm of blasts at him.

"It's over, Hedstrom! You were just delaying the inevitable," Fallon bitterly taunts. "The only thing that awaits you now is death itself!!"

Fallon's wicked laughter is heard throughout the Academy Ruins as Keenth struggles to realign himself for battle.

Before he could deliver the final blow, Fallon is interrupted by a massive wave of light-blue Auraen fired from above. In his anger, he directs his focus to the person responsible for the ambush.

"You dare knock on death's door," Fallon shouts. "Well? Speak for yourself, you damn coward!!"

The unknown warrior continues to bombard Fallon with waves of Auraen until they reach their limit.

Having reduced themselves to firing from one knee, while panting for air, the individual finally reveals themself.

"This is your chance!" Kendra shouts. "Do it now, Keenth. NOW!!"

With those words, Keenth immediately launches himself into the air, flying through the smoke. Fallon looks up in astonishment as Keenth's Auraen miraculously flares to its most vigorous heights yet again.

"What in the world is going on with his Auraen?? It isn't simply increasing...But it is flickering...As if...No, that's impossible," Fallon surmises as he increases the energy output of his armor.

"This is nothing at all to me. All of the power in the world doesn't mean a thing if the user is inexperienced," he continues to himself. "All I have to do is strike the instant before he releases his attack. With all of his strength focused on his sword, his defenses will be lowered."

One of Fallon's main power generators explodes then, having hit its limit. He attempts to remedy this, but a massive boom is heard as Keenth's sword is surrounded by an intensely sharp, blue Auraen.

"Well, you're up early. Is there something on your mind, son?"

"It's about this sword that you gave me...I don't think I'm ready for it."

"Not ready? Nonsense! You're my boy, aren't you? You were born for this!"

"I don't know, Dad. Part of me just feels too afraid to have something like this."

"I get it and that's natural. But! As Larkin M. Hedstrom is my name, I swear that you'll overcome those fears one day."

"Do you really think so, Dad?"

"Absolutely! You're a special one, son. Your mom and I were blessed with gifts and I expect big things from you in the future."

"The future? Why are you thinking that far ahead, Dad?"

"Because just like your mom, I won't be around forever. There will come a time when you'll have to decide the type of person you'll be. Don't let the world choose for you."

"It sounds like a lot to think about..."

"It is, but you already have everything you need to press forward. There's more of the world for you to see outside of Colonia. I just pray that, when necessary, you'll use your abilities to help others."

"Say Dad...You said I have everything I need, right? How will I know what kind of abilities I have?"

"Keenth, you have your whole life ahead of you to know what kind of person you'll turn out to be. But your power, a gift from your parents to you, is a particularly outstanding one. Remember this and remember it well, Keenth. Your power is—"

Light continues to erupt from Keenth's blade as it crashes down, ripping through Fallon's armor. With both feet firmly on the ground, Keenth shouts one word to the heavens as his opponent howls in anguish.

"RAIZEN!!!"

A gargantuan blade of thunder discharges from Keenth's sword, completely obliterating half of the Academy Ruins. Having used all of his power, Keenth collapses to the ground.

With his sword destroyed in the attack, Fallon's mask cracks in half and slowly falls as he looks down at the gaping hole where his abdomen used to be.

"I see...So it really came down to this," Fallon says. "So, their strength was able to reach these heights, after all..."

"Still, I will see this through...Whether it is the last thing I do," Fallon bitterly declares, using the last of his strength to aim his crossbow at Keenth's head. "One way or another, I will fulfill my legacy."

"To what end?" James weakly asks, making his way toward them. "Is this really where you want your legacy to end? Killing off the one who defeated you in an act of spite?"

"You don't know what you're talking about, James. The battle isn't over until the last warrior falls."

"He's just a boy, damn it! Neither of us will survive for much longer. Do you really want your last act in this world to be something as despicable as this, David?"

"...Then what do you suggest instead?"

"J-just leave him be, David. After all of this, after everything that he's gone through, he's earned that much. Please just be the bigger person and let him go."

"Let him go? To what end? The world won't nearly be so accepting towards someone with power like this. If anything, taking him out of his misery right now is probably for the best."

"I'm sure he'll certainly have challenges ahead. There will probably be suffering and pain that he will have to face too. But it isn't our place to decide for him; it's up to him to choose how he lives his life."

"I see...So you're really determined for him to live on, aren't you, James? Keenth Hedstrom...Paul Fehren...You two really turned out to be exceptional ones, after all."

*

"Wake up, Tortuga! This is W-NJFM with our top story. After being rocked with massive power outages throughout all three regions and reports of attacks from a rogue militia, we've received confirmation that the unknown assailants have been defeated.

"I don't know about you, but that's pretty good news to wake up to. So, go out and enjoy yourselves, people! We've lived to see another day, and if there's anything to take from this, it's that we shouldn't take life for granted!

"That's all for now, folks! We'll follow up with an official statement from the Tortuga High Council herself, Madam Chambers at 10AM, so stay tuned!"

"Where do I even start?" Kendra thinks to herself. "Lady Aida told me that Benjamin and the others were able to defend our village as promised, with Richard eventually joining in as well. Beth and Cory left early in the morning, so the fellas were stuck with Lady Aida's wrath for battling so recklessly."

"Cory, in typical fashion, went back into the forest. She promised she would come back to visit. What a sweetheart that girl is. I can't wait to see her again. I'll be sure to talk to Lady Aida about throwing a huge dinner for everyone sometime soon."

"Beth made it back to the Tortugan Capital City, where she was greeted with open arms by Madam Chambers and damn near hugged to death by her friend, Aya. It's good to know that she has support out there. Maybe I should pay her a visit and thank her in person before I make my way out to home."

"That's pretty much what Lady Aida filled me in on. I guess all that leaves is you," Kendra tells Keenth as he begins to open his eyes.

"K-Kendra? Where are we?" Keenth asks with his head still resting on Kendra's lap. "How long was I out for?"

"Hmm...I'd say about twelve hours. You really pushed yourself earlier. It isn't much, but I found some dorms that were still intact for us to rest in. It's truly a miracle the Academy is still standing after everything that went down last night."

"Yeah, we got pretty lucky after all. Come on, there's somewhere I want to take you," Keenth replies as he picks himself up. "Hopefully it wasn't damaged too much between everything that's been going on."

Keenth and Kendra take their time to carefully navigate through the Academy until they eventually reach his old room. Fortunately, it was mostly left intact, despite the odds. Kendra begins asking Keenth about his space, but he remains silent as he reflects on the events leading up to this moment.

"It's been quite the journey, Kendra. I'm grateful to be standing here but, I don't know, something isn't sitting right with me."

"Really? You've made your way from hell and back. I wasn't even here for half of it, but I know that you've worked so hard to get to where you are. I'm proud of you for that and you should be too. Appreciate the good that you've seen as you've gone through your path."

"I understand all of that, I really do, but there were things that Fallon said that I can't shake out of my head. Before you start, I know I should take his words with a grain of salt. But I felt that had it not been for certain people in my life, then there's a chance that I would have ended up like him too."

"If you ask me, I think that there's way more to us than the people we associate ourselves with, Keenth. I truly believe that you decided to be the type of person you were a long time ago. It was just a matter of you realizing that on your own. Took you a bit, but you got there."

"Thanks, Kendra. I appreciate that. Well, anyway, here's my room. You probably won't believe me, but I swear it normally isn't this dirty."

"I was going to give you grief about how dusty it is, but I decided to give you a pass because you barely have a roof over your head. What you need to do, my friend, is switch your clothes. Let's see what kind of horrible attempts at fashion you have here."

"But, Kendra, aren't you the same person who's basically worn nothing but purple cloaks every time I've seen you?"

"Hush, you wouldn't get it! Now hurry and wear this before I choke you with it!"

"Jeez...I must've struck a nerve," Keenth responds as he puts on a dark blue hoodie before slinging the Fehrenblade over his shoulder. "Great, it still fits like a glove!"

"You sound surprised. It's probably because you've lost your focus, haven't you? Nice try, but I'm not one to let my apprentices get all soft and lazy! You know the drill. We'll use a tougher version of my training program as soon as we get back to Azoco."

"About that, Kendra," Keenth explains. "I've decided not to head back to the village."

"I see. So, it's time for you to head back to your real home then?"

"Hey...I'll always consider Azoco village like a second home. But no, I'm not going to Colonia either. I think I'm going to spend time in Tortuga for a while."

"Is there any particular reason for you to do this? I figure you're a few years too young to be having some sort of a quarter-life crisis."

"Everyone that I've met along the way has changed my life forever.

I feel as though I still have so much to learn from Hasania and its people. If I was able to grow as much as I have these past couple of months, I can only imagine what's next for me."

"Alright, sounds good to me."

"Really? You aren't upset with me or anything?"

"Do I really look like the type of person who would get upset over something like...On second thought, don't answer that. Look, I completely support your decision. If it came from the heart, then I'm all for it. Just be sure to take care of yourself, okay?"

"You already know, Kendra. I'll be sure to drop in here and there to see how you guys are doing. If I run into Cory and the others, I'll let them know you said hello."

"No, you won't because I didn't! Tell them if they are wondering how we're doing, then they are always welcome to see for themselves."

"Will do! Well, I guess this is goodbye for now...Isn't it, Kendra?"

"I suppose you're right," Kendra agrees as she softly kisses Keenth on the forehead. "It goes without saying, but we'll always be here for you if there's anything you need."

"Thank you...Thank you, and the same here. Hey, since most of the Academy is destroyed, I think I'm going to go ahead and make my way out of this window. It's always something that I wanted to do, but—"

"I'm going to keep my comments to myself with that one, but I think you should take this with you," Kendra says, handing a photo over to Keenth.

"It's a picture of you and your friend, Paul, that I found on your desk. You should really hold onto this with care."

"Wow, would you look at that? Thanks, I appreciate it. Be easy, Kendra."

Keenth reflects fondly on the memories of his Academy days with Paul, his journey with Cory, the camaraderie shared with Benjamin and Beth, and Kendra's friendship throughout his time in Azoco village.

"Thank you for everything," Keenth thinks to himself as he leaps out of his window, dashing through the sky.

"Hasania! A new adventure awaits!!"

ACKNOWLEDGEMENTS

Hello, and thanks for reading *Fighter's Fever: The Metallic Siege*!

The process of writing out this story has been an absolute blast, and I hope you enjoyed reading this story just as well.

This is dedicated to those who showed me that anything is possible if you follow your dreams.

The mentorship, editing, and design help that I received was crucial in bringing this story to life.

Many thanks to those involved and for the support throughout the years; I truly appreciate each and every one of you.

Last but not least, a special note to my girls: The sky is the limit only if you allow it to be.

-R. Nazaire (MrNazaire)

ABOUT THE AUTHOR

Ricardo Nazaire is a writer born in New Jersey, and raised in the New York Metropolitan Area.

Constantly aspiring to faithfully reflect his experiences across the country and abroad Africa, Central America, and Europe, he wishes to share stories using the people he has met along the way as inspiration.

Aside from traveling, Ricardo enjoys improving his craft, pitching underappreciated jokes, and looking towards the next adventure.

For more information about the author and the story, please follow him at **twitter.com/MrNazaire**

www.ingramcontent.com/pod-product-compliance
Lightning Source LLC
Chambersburg PA
CBHW060130130626
46556CB00006B/2294